GROWING PANGS

GROWING PANGS

KATHRYN ORMSBEE

ILLUSTRATED BY

MOLLY BROOKS

WITH COLOR BY BEX GLENDINING AND ELISE SCHUENKE

RANDOM HOUSE 🏠 NEW YORK

Text copyright © 2022 by Kathryn Ormsbee
Jacket art and interior illustrations copyright © 2022 by Molly Brooks

All rights reserved. Published in the United States by Random House Children's Books, a division of Penguin Random House LLC, New York.

Random House and the colophon are registered trademarks of Penguin Random House LLC. RH Graphic with the book design is a trademark of Penguin Random House LLC.

Photographs on pp. 243 and 245 from the personal collection of Kathryn Ormsbee, used by permission.

Visit us on the Web! rhcbooks.com

Educators and librarians, for a variety of teaching tools, visit us at RHTeachersLibrarians.com

Library of Congress Cataloging-in-Publication Data is available upon request.
ISBN 978-0-593-30128-9 (hardcover) | ISBN 978-0-593-30131-9 (trade pbk.)
ISBN 978-0-593-30129-6 (lib. bdg.) | ISBN 978-0-593-30130-2 (ebook)

Interior design by Molly Brooks and April Ward

MANUFACTURED IN CHINA
10 9 8 7 6 5 4 3 2 1
First Edition

To Beth Phelan, who has been
an agent extraordinaire these
eight years and who encouraged me
to try something new and scary,
like writing a graphic novel

—K.O.

For my parents

—M.B.

PART ONE
Summer
CAMP ALDRIDGE

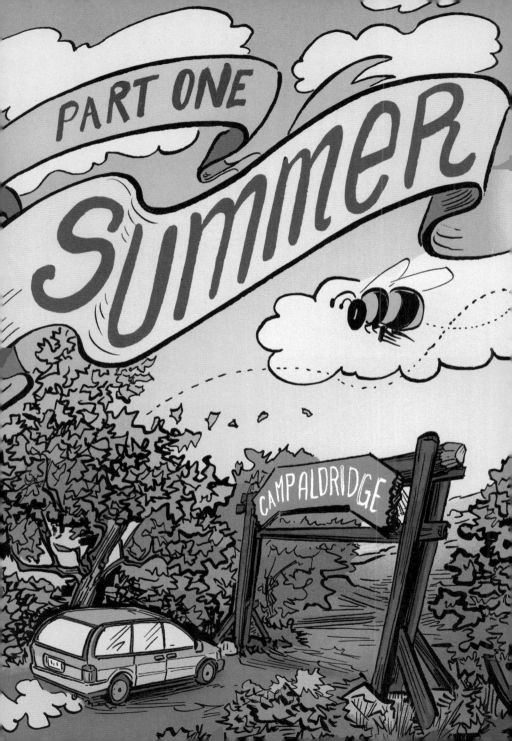

It was summer break, and I had so many plans.
Almost all of them involved my best friend, Kacey.
Katie!
giggle

Kacey and I had met two years earlier at our weekly homeschool co-op.
WELCOME BACK, BLUEGRASS HOMESCHOOL CO-OP!
Katie
Kacey
We hit it off right away.
Hey! Our names sound cool together. Like a band.
We both loved books.
Have you read the new Royal Diaries book about Anastasia?
YES. I wonder if she really escaped the Bolsheviks.
Right? She could still be alive in France or someplace!
You're NEVER FULLY DRESSED WITHOUT A SMILE!
We were obsessed with the musical *Annie*.

And we were both homeschooled.

BLUEGRASS HOMESCHOOL CO-OP

estoy estamos
estás estáis
está están

So I didn't feel like the weirdo homeschooled kid when Kacey and I hung out.

Wait. You two don't go to *real* school?

WEIRDOS!

HAHAHAHAHA

I did school at home for most of the week, but Fridays were co-op days.

That's when I went to classes like Spanish, art, drama, and gym with other homeschoolers.

After co-op, I would go to Kacey's house, or she would come to mine, and we would record our very own made-up radio show.
That's the weather report for this week.
And now for a commercial break from our sponsor.
Or we'd play our favorite computer game, *RollerCoaster Tycoon*.
Or work on our top-secret original script for *Annie the Musical: The Sequel*.
Annie
the musical
(the Sequel)
Songs—
·Another day in NYC
·Ms. Hannigan Strikes
Or we'd jump for hours on the trampoline . . .
Whoa!
. . . and only stop to munch on sour candy.

Kacey made trips to the mall with my mom and my sister, Ashley, super fun.
Operation Friendship Necklace.
CANDY TOWN
We gotta find something that's one of a kind!
Jeni's
Jewelry & Accessories

Nuh-uh.
Yes.
BEST
FRIENDS
Best friends.
Forever!

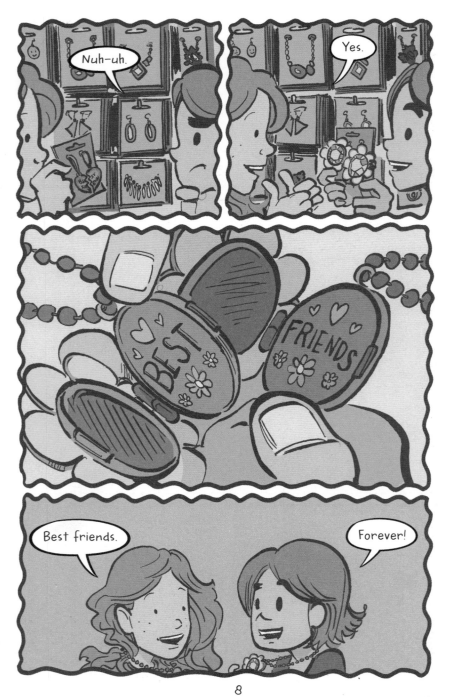

Homeschool co-op let out for summer break in May. But that didn't mean Kacey and I stopped hanging out.
I was thinking—
Lemme guess: PICNIC.
Summer meant even more adventures together.
This was a great idea.
What a perfect day.
By the way, I've been meaning to tell you about . . .
THIS!
CAMP ALDRIDGE

I know older kids from church who've gone. They say it's *awesome*.

And there's a giant pool?

Uh-huh. And a zip line and a campfire, *and* there's a big talent show at the end of the week.

It sounds *really* cool.

When I asked my parents about Camp Aldridge . . .

. . . they said I could go!

But a few weeks later . . .

You've been quiet tonight, Katiebug.

I'm a little worried, I guess.

About camp.

That makes sense.

It does?

Sure. Overnight camp is a big deal.

It's only natural you're nervous.

Dad and I will be a phone call away.

And you'll have Kacey there with you.

Yeah.

Hey, um . . . Ashley?

Uh–huh.

You've been to camp before, right?

Yeah.

It's not a big deal.

You'll forget you were nervous after the first day.

Okay.

I wanted to talk more about it.

But I didn't want Ashley thinking I was scared.

Ashley and I used to hang out more.
I'm Queen of the Animal Kingdom!
Our armies shall decide, Eagle.

But now Ashley was in high school and doing grown-up stuff.
Weez
Donate

She moved her stuff from our bathroom into the creepy bathroom in the basement, so she could have her own space.

I wanted to be like Ashley one day.

Pretty and cool and confident.

Right now, though?

Compared to Ashley, I felt like a little kid.

But Camp Aldridge was a chance to prove I was mature.

I can do this.

Miss Mary Mack Mack Mack!
The big day arrived, and we were off!
All dressed in BLACK BLACK BLACK!

With silver buttons, buttons, buttons!
CLAP
CLAP

All down her back, back, ba—
Whoops!
giggle
My stomach feels funny.
Maybe I'm already homesick?

I couldn't swat away a buzzing feeling in my brain.
BZZZZZ
BZZZZZZ
What if you miss home *too* much?
BZZ BZZZ
So much that you can't fall asleep at night?
What if you do something super embarrassing in front of the whole camp?
BZZZ
Or you get sick, and Mom's not there to take care of you?

This wasn't the first time I'd gotten buzzing thoughts.
They'd started a few years ago.
Lately, though, I'd been getting them more and more.
BZZ BZZ
BZZZ
BZZ
BZZZ
They told me what to do, like a big, buzzing bully.
You gotta make your worries stop.
Move that zipper.
BZZZZ

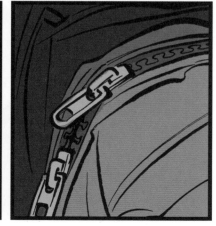

Ziiiip
If I moved the zipper, camp would be fun. Nothing bad would happen.
ONE Zip
TWO Zip
THREE Zip
You just have to move it three more times.
ONE
TWO
Hey.

What're you doing?

Um. Nothing.

Okay, cool. I thought your backpack was broken.

How bad would *that* be on our first day of camp?

Yeah. Totally.

I left my backpack alone after that.

BZzz BZzz

But the buzzing thoughts didn't go away.

CAMP ALDRIDGE
WELCOME, CAMPERS!
DROP-OFF

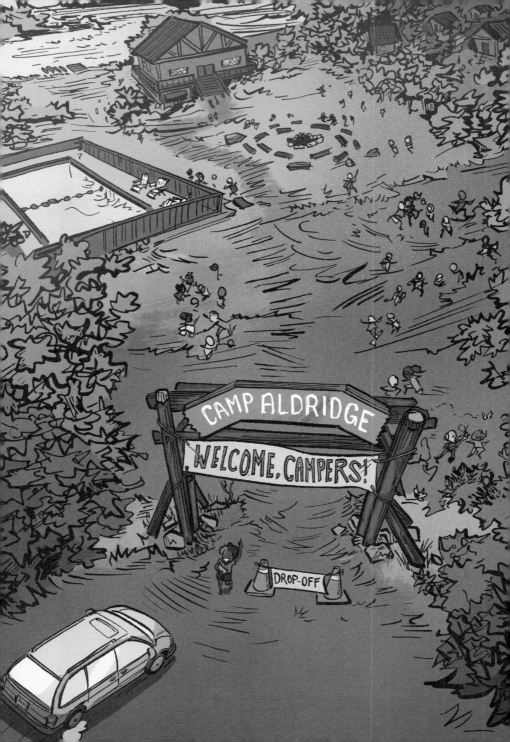

Welcome to Camp Aldridge! We're so happy you're here.

EEEEEE♡!E!E!E!

Could you take a picture of us?
Sure!
I want to remember our very first minute at camp.
CAMP RIDGE
Thanks!
No problem. Now let's go check out your cabin.

You've arrived a little late in the day, so there's only one bunk left.
That's okay!
Yeah, we're best friends. It'll be fun to share a bunk bed.
Home sweet home!
The other girls are out exploring, but you'll get to meet them tonight.

I call bottom bunk!

Okay, Katie, that means you get . . .

. . . the top bunk.

gulp.

I'll let you girls get settled. Dinner is at the mess hall in thirty minutes!

Hey, Kacey?

Would you maybe wanna switch beds?

Why?

I couldn't admit that I was scared I'd fall off in the middle of the night.

Poof!

I'm just used to sleeping closer to the ground.

BZZ BZZ

Well, then it's more of an adventure to sleep on the top bunk, right?

Yeah, I guess so.

BZZ

Let's head over to the mess hall!

The counselors sing before dinner, and it's *hilarious.*

Oh, yeah! Um . . .

You go ahead. I'll catch up.

If you're sure. I'll save a spot for you.

The buzzing thoughts were bad.

They told me that if I made my bed *just so* . . .

Tuck!

BZZZ

Tuck

. . . I wouldn't fall off in the middle of the night.

29

I knew thoughts like that didn't make sense. How could making my bed stop me from falling out of it?
But doing what the buzzing thoughts said to do?
Poof!
That made them go away at least.

CLOMP CLOMP
The buzzing thoughts seemed to always show up when I felt scared or uncomfortable.
But I hadn't told anyone about them.
MESS HALL
POOL
There were already plenty of things that made me different from other kids.
Stuff that makes me Different
red hair
• young for my grade
• homeschooled
• supercrooked teeth (going to get braces next month)
tons of freckles

I didn't want to add buzzing thoughts to that list.

I had to keep cool and not act like a kid. I had to—

HEY!

TAP

M—me?

Yeah, you.

My name's Delaney. You headed to dinner?

Yeah! I'M Katie.

Delaney is such a cool name.

So what grade are you going into?
Sixth.
Sweet! Me too. Where do you go?
Uh-oh. One of the things that makes me different . . .
I go to school in Lexington.
That's not exactly a lie.
Oh. I live in Bowling Green.
That's pretty far from here.
Yeah, it's basically Tennessee.
MESS HALL

So what's your favorite band?
Mine is *NSYNC.
I wonder where Kacey is.
You gotta choose an alliance: *NSYNC or Backstreet Boys.
But Backstreet Boys suck.
Lance is pretty cute, but Joey is so old. Like, a dinosaur. And then there's Chris and JC, who I'm just like "meh" about.
Sooo, who do you like?
Whoa. Delaney cusses. I'm not allowed to say "suck."
And I don't know any members of *NSYNC.

I like musicals.
You know, like *The Phantom of the Opera*? Or *Annie*?
Huh. Interesting.
Who're you looking for?
My friend . . .
. . . KACEY!
Isn't this place *awesome*?
I grabbed you a glow-in-the-dark lanyard! They were running out.
Thanks!
Delaney, this is my best friend, Kacey.
So you two go to the same school?

Actually, we're . . .
Oh no. Don't say it.
. . . homeschooled.
NOOOOOOOOOOOO
Oh. That's . . . interesting.
I got the feeling that when Delaney said "interesting" she really meant "uncool."
Giggle
HA HA

But Delaney *was* cool.

That's the best spot in the house!

Hey, Delaney!

What's up, Delaney?

A&F

And confident.

We were here first, dudes. Back off!

37

She knew lots of stuff I didn't, about music and movies and *life*.

I'll have to show you how I do mascara.

It's a trick I learned from *Cosmopolitan*.

And oh my God, do you ever think about how we could be in a real-life *Friday the 13th*?

Like, Jason could be watching us right now.

Delaney can watch R-rated movies?

I call it EXTREME FIZZ. You gotta put in every single soda flavor.

Ew, gross!

. . . but cool.

You know what would be awesome? Synchronized swimming in the pool!

Oooh, yeah. We should try it.

Sounds fine, I guess.

So homeschooling. Does that mean you do school in your pajamas?

No. I get dressed, just like "normal" kids.

Interesting . . .

I can't believe you've never seen *Scary Movie*. It's, like, a classic.

Like, you *do* have a TV, right?

Of course! I watch lots of movies and TV shows.

So have you seen the trailer for the *Lord of the Rings* movie?

Yeah! I can't wait for it to come out.

But I'll have to get special permission from my parents to watch it.

We could be our own fellowship.
The fellowship of . . . the bracelet!
S-s-sure!
Awesome!

HA HA HA HA HA HA HA
HA HA
HA HA HA
HA HA HA
HA HA HA HA HA HA HA
See ya!
MESS HALL
Bye!

I don't like Delaney. She's too loud.
I think she's fun.
Because she gave you a friendship bracelet, huh?
She was just being nice.
You can't have *two* best friends.
I've only got one of these.
You're my best friend, Kacey. Nothing's gonna change that.
Best friends forever.

I still wanted Kacey and Delaney to get along.
All for one!
And one for all!
For us to be like the Three Musketeers.
But pretty soon I figured out . . .
. . . that wasn't going to happen.

Camp Aldridge was jam-packed with fun things to do.
AHHH AHHH!
ZIP-LINING
ART
CAMPFIRE
Camp Aldridge, always in our hearts!
Aren't you glad you didn't turn on the light?
MUSIC
CRAFTS
HIKING
Vrr

ZZZZZ
BZZZ BZZZZ
Even though I got homesick every so often . . .
ZZZZz
CANNONBALL
8FT
. . . it was nothing a little camp fun couldn't fix.
My sister, Ashley, says I should enjoy stuff like this while I can.
8Ft
She says you can't eat marshmallow *anything* when you have braces.
That sucks. You nervous about getting them?
Kind of. I'm mainly worried I'll look weird.
Oh. You *definitely* will.
But if anyone can pull off a brace face, it's you.

You're spending too much time with Delaney.

We're just hanging out.

But camp was my idea.

You should be spending more time with me.

If you're friends with Delaney, you're, like, betraying our friendship.

I hadn't meant to betray Kacey.

I'd just been having fun with Delaney, too.

Check it out. It's the new Weezer album.

My sister likes them!

She plays them in her bathroom all the time.

She's got the same Walkman as you, too.

It was different, being friends with Delaney.

She was more like Ashley than like Kacey.

More . . . grown-up.

Well, how come you don't like them?

Too deep for you!

What if Delaney thinks I'm *not* grown-up? Not cool enough?

I forgot you like *musicals*. Cute, fluffy stuff like that.

No! I like this kind of music, too.

I just have to save up for my own CDs, and that can take a while.

Well, you can borrow mine whenever.

That's what the fellowship of the bracelet is for.

49

The buzzing thoughts wouldn't leave me alone.

They told me I would feel better if I did certain things.

Like retie my shoes, even when they were perfectly tied.

Go on without me! I'll catch up!

. . . eight, nine, *ten.*

Whoa! Easy there.

Or tap the dispensers a certain number of times when I was making an Extreme Fizz.

I knew deep down that those buzzing thoughts were silly.

50

BZZ
BZ
But sometimes they were all I could hear.
ZZZZZZZZZZ
BZZZ
BZZZ
BZZZZ
BZZ

CAMP ALDRIDGE TALENT SHOW

On the last day of camp, Kacey and I sang a duet.

YOU'RE Never fully dressed without a smile!

But she wasn't totally happy with me.

GOODBYE, CAMPERS

Delaney and I were bummed, too.

I wish you didn't live so far from Lexington.

It majorly sucks.

Call me whenever.

Yeah. And if homeschool kids get school pictures, send me one.

I wanna see what you look like as a brace face.

Remember: The fellowship of the bracelet will endure!

53

Kacey and I wouldn't be riding home together.

Her family was going to Canada for three weeks.

That meant Kacey would be gone on the first day of homeschool co-op.

And she still seemed mad about Delaney.

I hoped that when she got home from vacation, everything would go back to normal.

Have fun up north!

Poof!

She was wearing her necklace at least.

On the ride home, I opened and shut my locket ten times in a row.

CLiCK

BZZz

You're an official overnight camper.

It's old hat now!

The buzzing thoughts told me that if I did that, I wouldn't lose my best friend.

CLick

CLick

BZZZzzz

I was home, and it was the end of summer.

Since Kacey wasn't around, I had lots of free time.

Sometimes I snuck into Ashley's room to look at her magazines.

Hmm.

Can I get a haircut before school starts?

Sure! Between your braces and your haircut, you'll be a whole new Katie.

A haircut would change everything.

I'd finally be as cool as Ashley and Delaney.

That weekend . . .

You must be Katie.

You want your hair chopped, huh?

Well, you gotta promise not to cry about it in the morning.

Promise.

SNIP!

SNIP

All right. Ready?

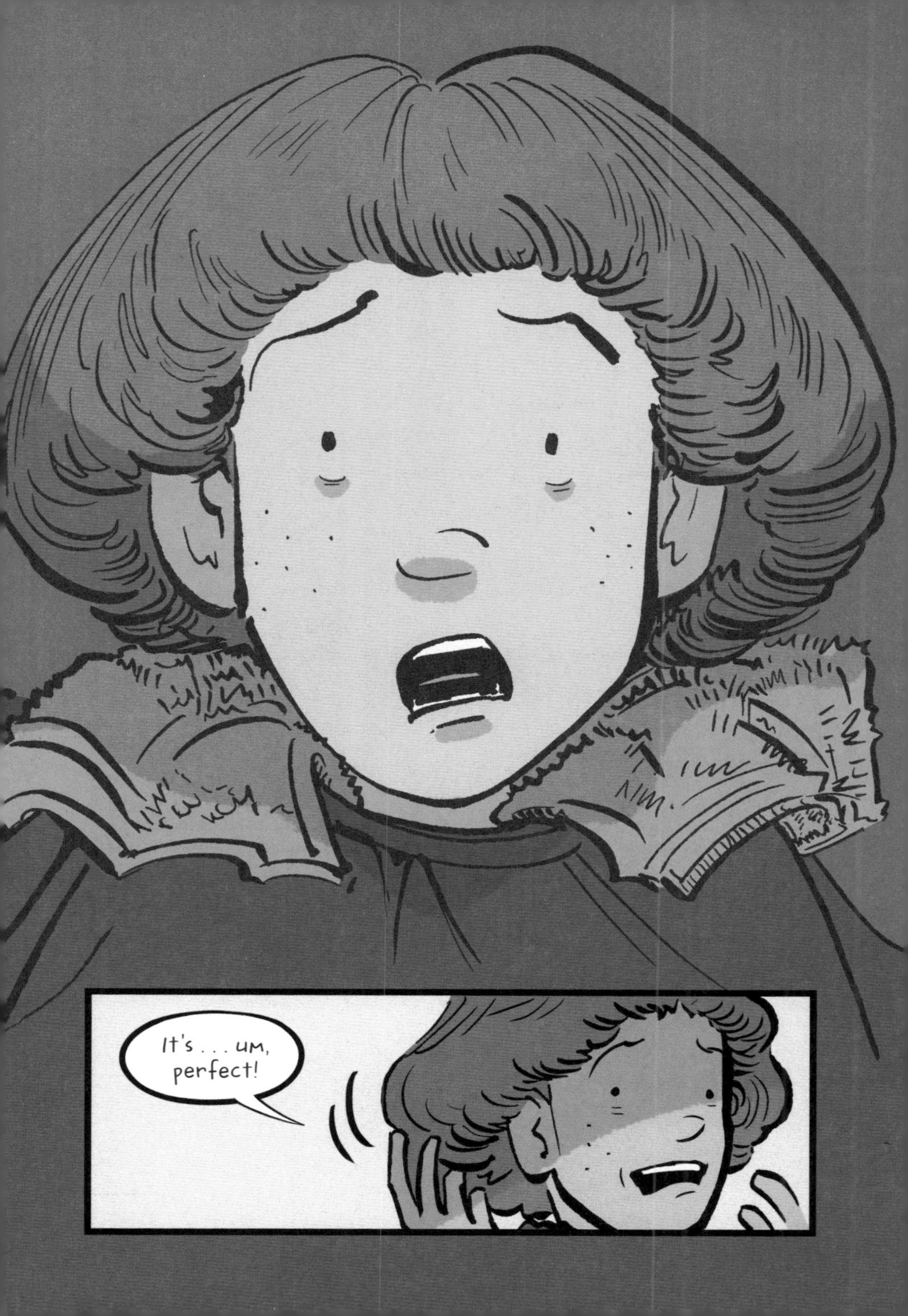
It's . . . um, perfect!

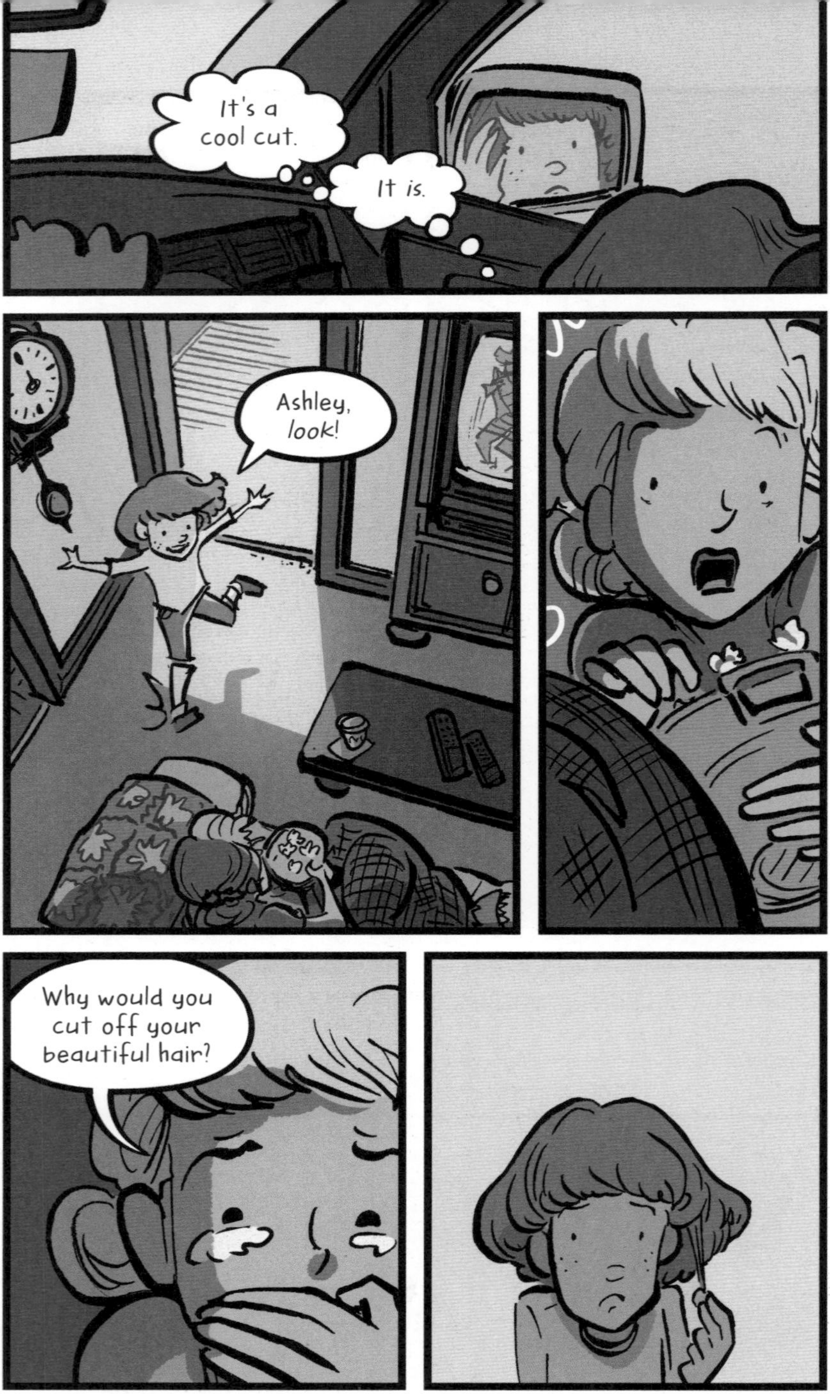
It's a cool cut.
It is.
Ashley, *look!*
Why would you cut off your beautiful hair?

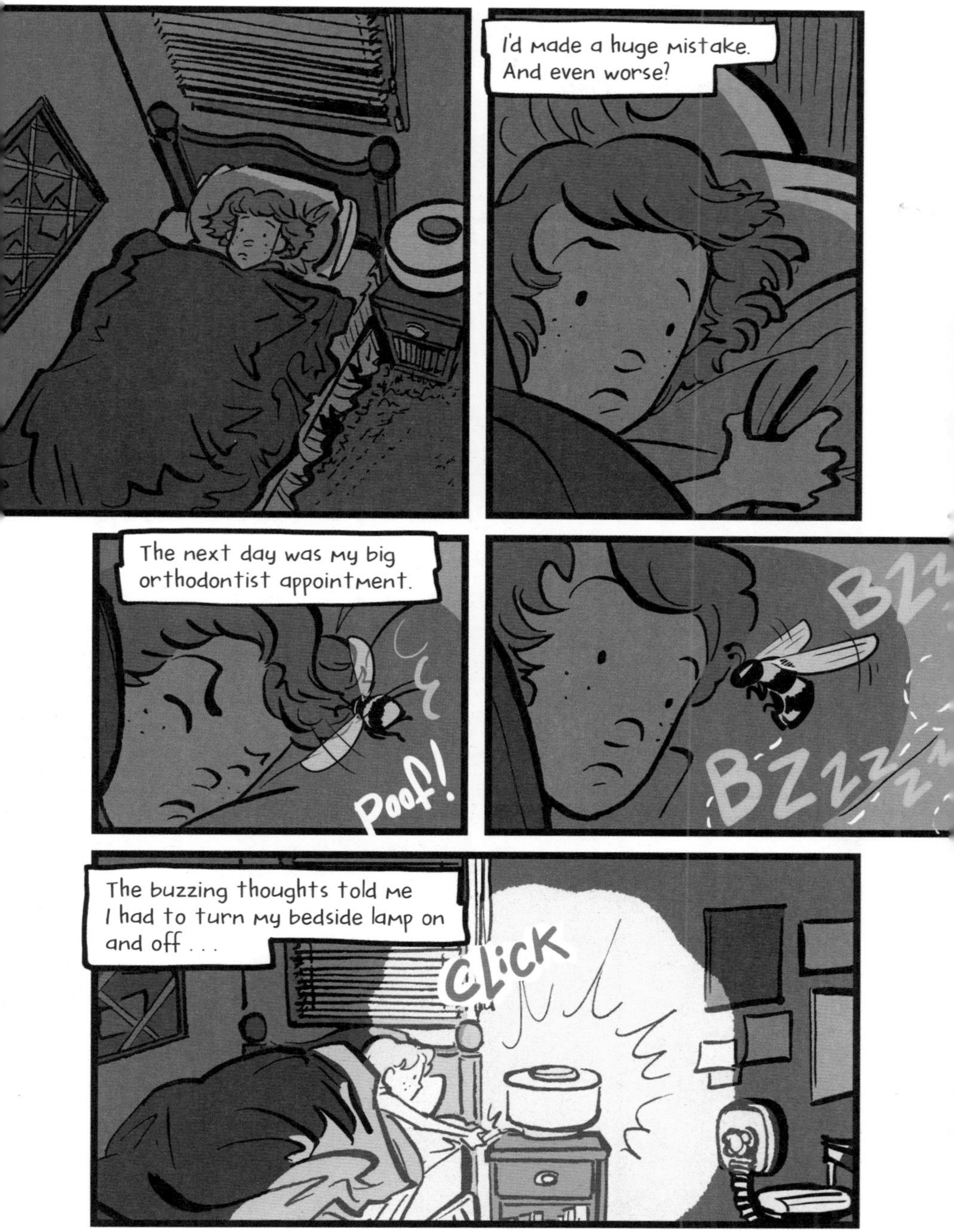
I'd made a huge mistake. And even worse?
The next day was my big orthodontist appointment.
Poof!
BZZZ
BZZZ
The buzzing thoughts told me I had to turn my bedside lamp on and off . . .
CLICK

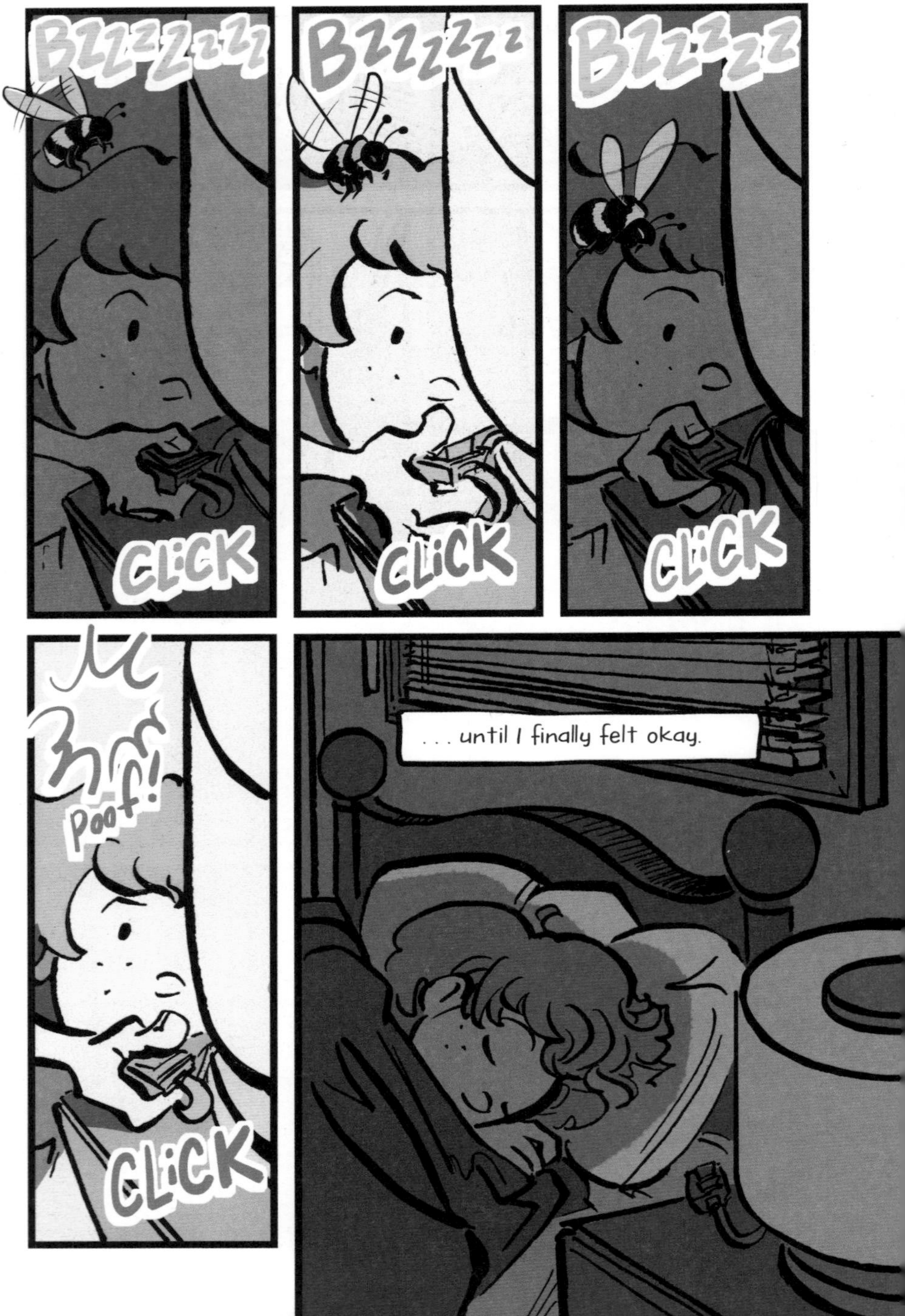
BZZZZZZZ
CLICK
BZZZZZZZ
CLICK
BZZZZZZ
CLICK
3mf!
poof!
CLICK
. . . until I finally felt okay.

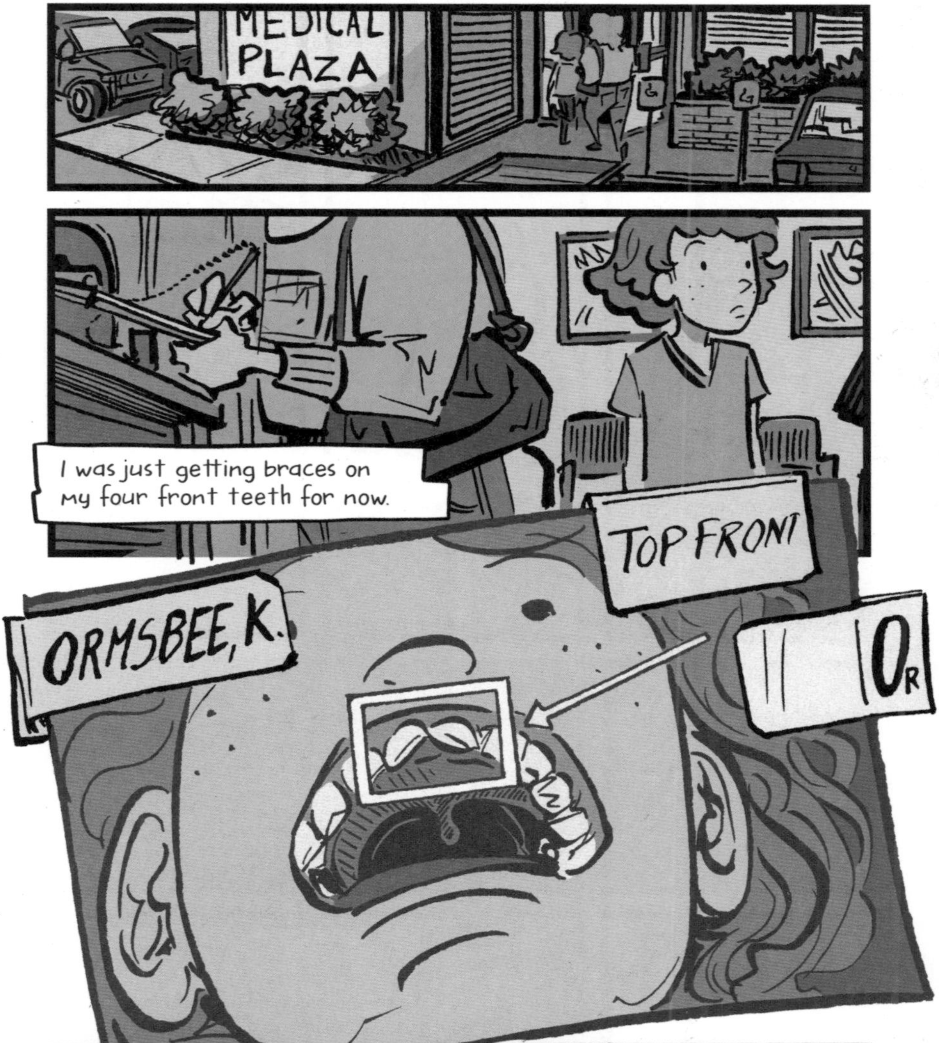
MEDICAL
PLAZA
I was just getting braces on my four front teeth for now.
TOP FRONT
ORMSBEE, K.
Katie?
Poof!

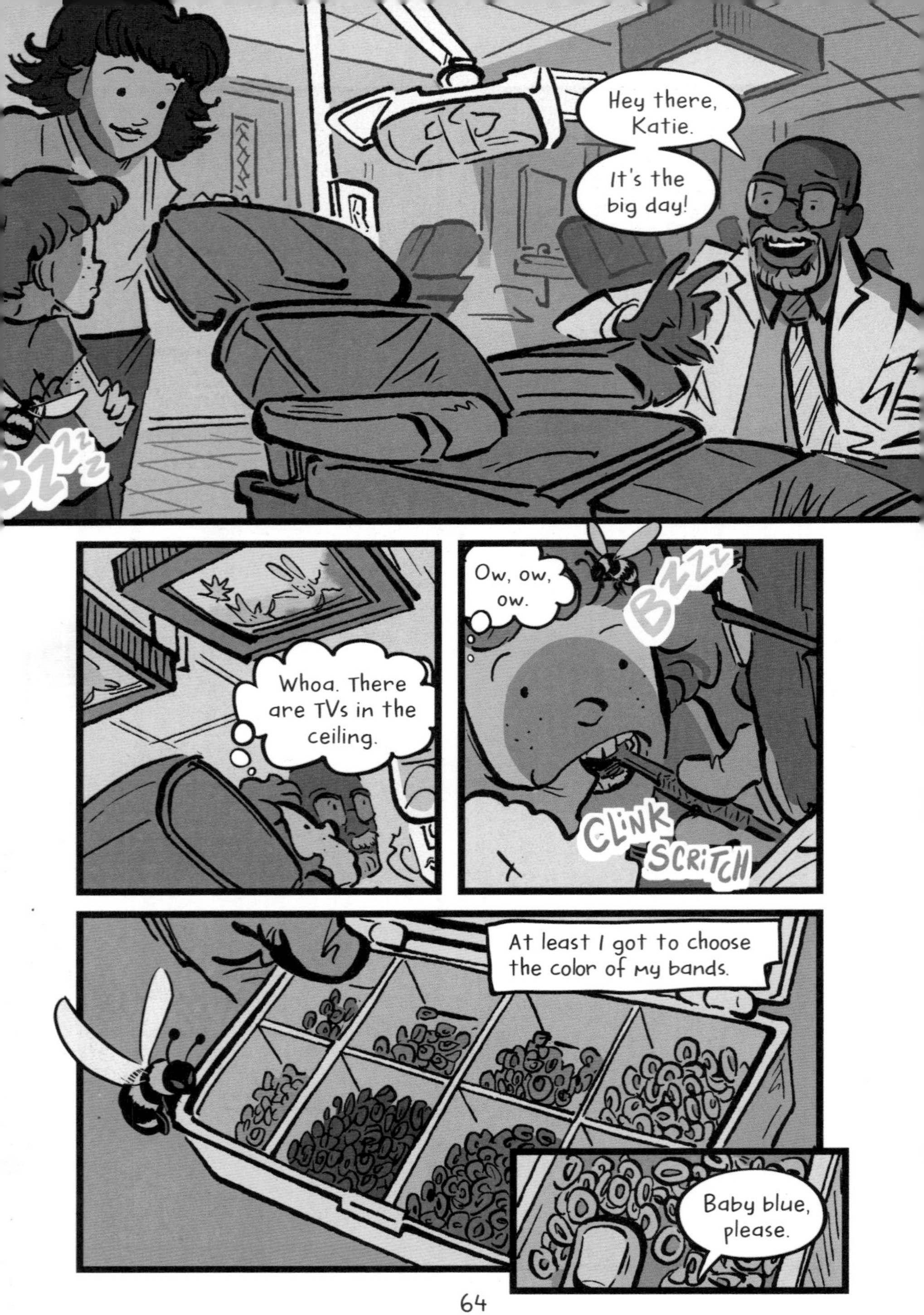
Hey there, Katie.
It's the big day!
BZZZZ
Whoa. There are TVs in the ceiling.
Ow, ow, ow.
BZZZ
CLINK
SCRITCH
At least I got to choose the color of my bands.
Baby blue, please.

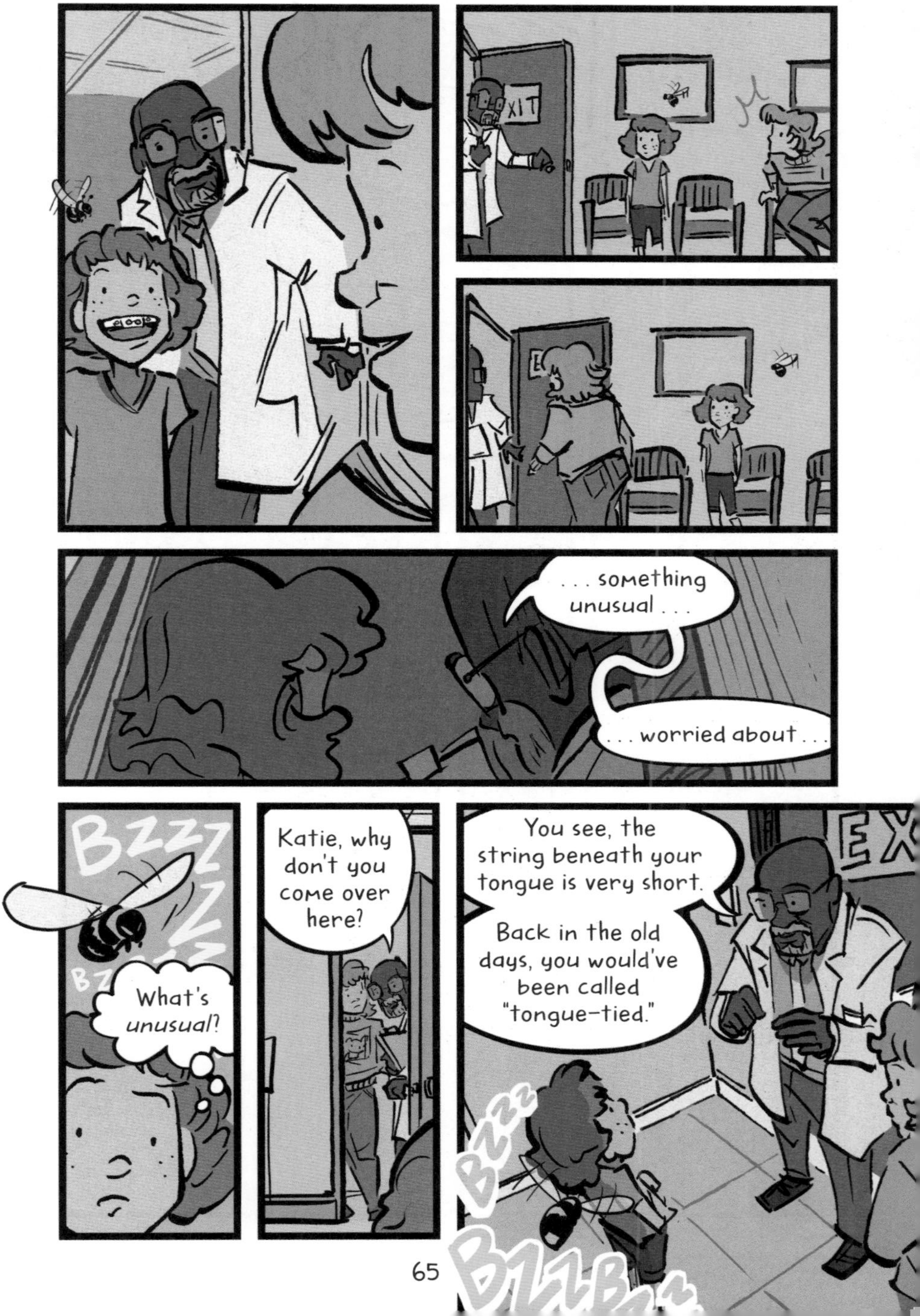
XIT
. . . something unusual . . .
. . . worried about . . .
Bzzz
Bz
What's *unusual*?
Katie, why don't you come over here?
You see, the string beneath your tongue is very short.
Back in the old days, you would've been called "tongue-tied."
EX
Bzzz
BZZB

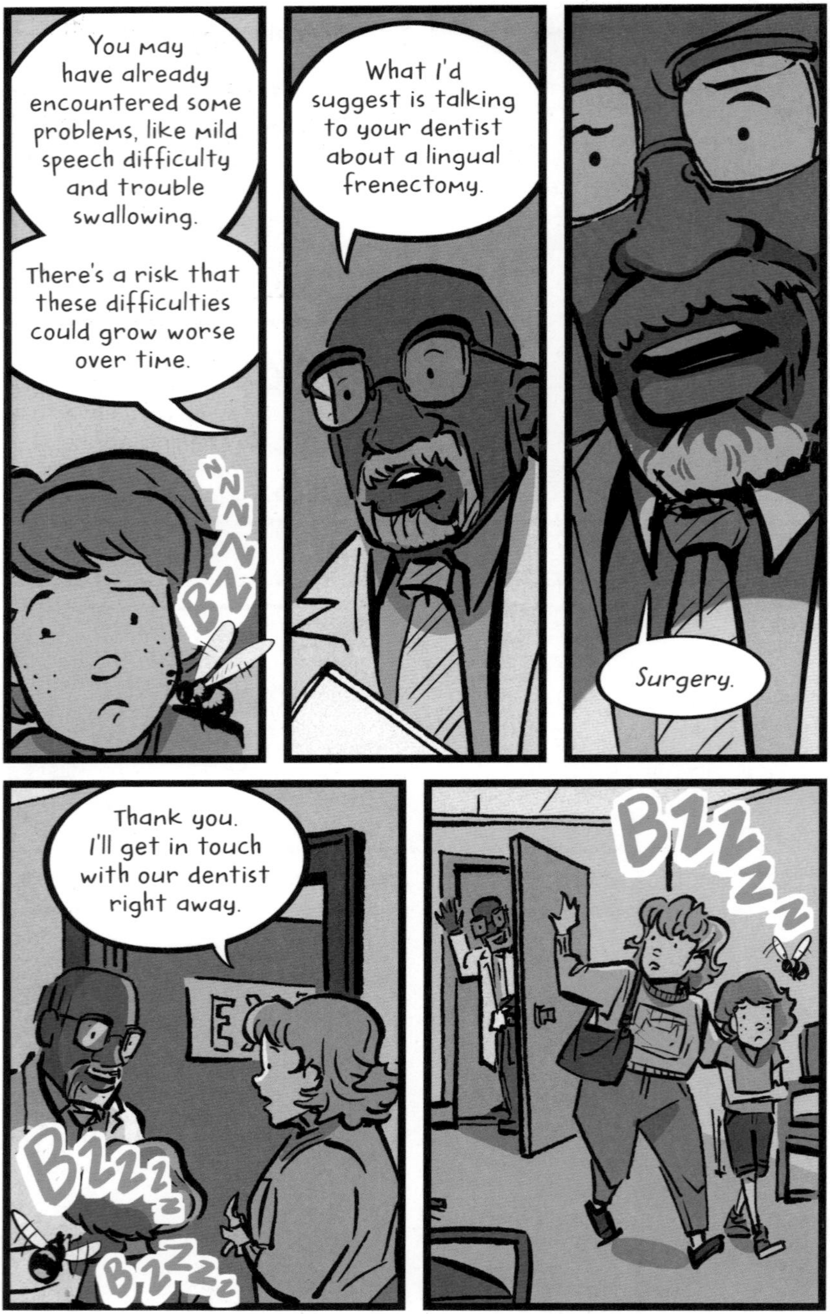
You may have already encountered some problems, like mild speech difficulty and trouble swallowing.
There's a risk that these difficulties could grow worse over time.
NNNNN
BZ
What I'd suggest is talking to your dentist about a lingual frenectomy.
Surgery.
Thank you. I'll get in touch with our dentist right away.
Bzzzz
Bzzzz
Bzzzz

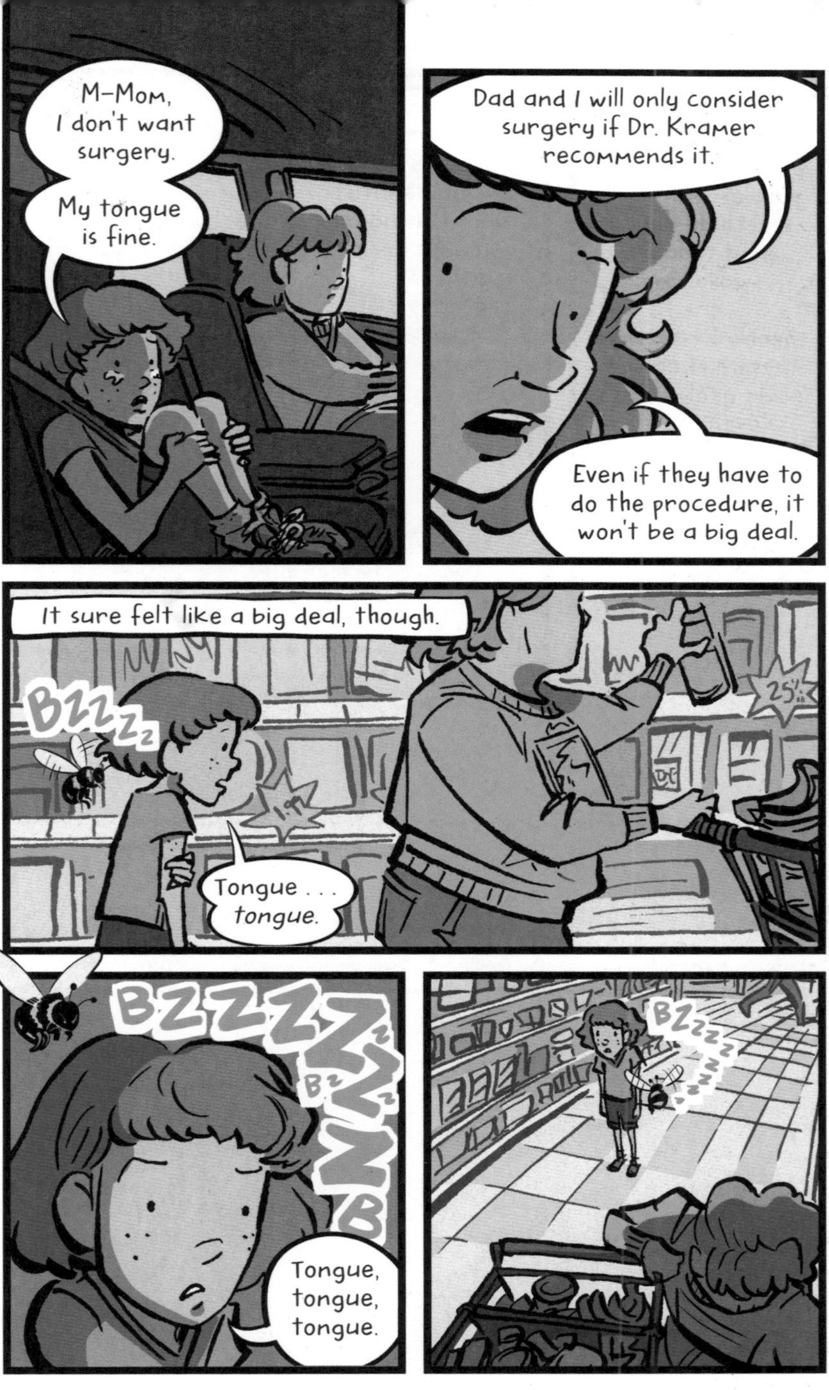
M–Mom, I don't want surgery.
My tongue is fine.
Dad and I will only consider surgery if Dr. Kramer recommends it.
Even if they have to do the procedure, it won't be a big deal.
It sure felt like a big deal, though.
Tongue . . . tongue.
Tongue, tongue, tongue.

The buzzing thoughts told me that if I whispered the word "tongue" enough, the surgery wouldn't happen.
UP TO 60% off
BUY 2 GET 1 50%
Tongue. Tongue. Tongue.
BZZZZZ
BZZZ BZZZ BZZZ BZZZ
Tongue.
Tongue, tongue.
BZZZZZZ
Poof
Are you ready for school, hon?
Yes, ma'am.
And where do you go?

I'm homeschooled.
Oh. I see.
That's *such* a disservice to your child. How will she learn to socialize?
Oh, I think she'll manage.
Have a nice day!

I'd met plenty of adults who seemed to think homeschooling was weird, or even bad.
How does she *socialize*?
Does she get out of the house much?
Do they just watch TV all day?
But other people will think it's strange.
It'll be a disadvantage to her in the real world.

I didn't think homeschooling was strange. And I definitely didn't stay inside all day, watching TV. I got to do all sorts of things.
4-H CLUB
I pledge my head to clearer thinking, my heart to greater loyalty . . .
GYMNASTICS
MUSIC LESSONS
CHURCH
TENNIS
HOMESCHOOL CO-OP
Bogotá, Colombia

Plus, I liked to work at my own pace at home.
And I didn't have to worry about homework at night.
I didn't think those adults knew what homeschooling was actually like for me.

My friends at the homeschool co-op did, though. I couldn't wait to see them again.
1995 BLUE GRASS HOMESCHOOL CO-OP
SCHOOL CO-OP
HOMESCHOC
YEARBOOK CLUB
You excited about co-op starting, Katiebug?
Yeah. Especially drama. We're going to do a holiday talent show, *and* Mrs. Navuluri is gonna announce the big end-of-the-year play.

I just wished Kacey was back from Canada.
TORONTO
Wish you were here! xo Kacey
Katie Ormsbee
KY
Co-op wouldn't be the same without her.
FRIENDS

PART TWO
FALL
CHILDREN'S THEATRE

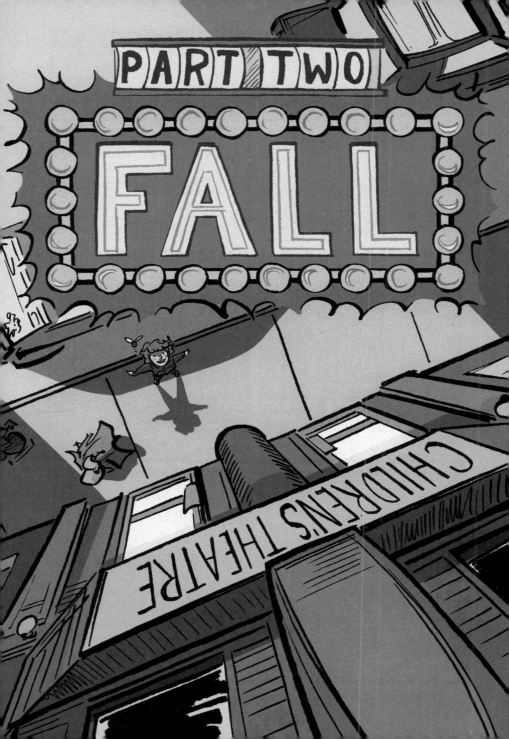

NNNN
First day of co-cop!
First day of middle school.
First day of—wait.
Is that . . .
A PIMPLE?

What's wrong?

On my FIRST DAY. I can't show my face like this!

Sure you can. Plenty of people your age get pimples. It's completely normal.

I bet even a few of your friends will have them.

Poof

It's not as bad as you think. People will hardly notice.

Bzzz

But to me, that pimple was my worst enemy.

Bzz Bzzz

Bzzzzz *Bzzz* *Bzz*

Haha! I'm gonna make sixth grade the *worst*.

I tried to focus on good things, like seeing my friends and filling my brand-new binder with notes.

Katie!

Hey!

Lauren
Megan ↓ Callie

No one said a thing about my pimple. They were all too excited about . . .

. . . the *new girl.*

This is Jaime! She just started homeschooling this year.

Nice to meet you.

We have the same binder!

Guess we both have good taste.

Oh, hey, they're starting opening ceremonies.

Wanna sit together?

Definitely. I can show you around since it's your first day.

I love theatre. I was in lots of plays at my old school.

We did a production of *A Midsummer Night's Dream* that was set in the 1920s, and I got to be a flapper named Helena.

That's so cool!

Jaime reminded me a little of Delaney: She was cool and outgoing, but she wasn't as . . . *intense.*

And she was homeschooled, so I didn't have to worry that she'd make fun of me or not understand.

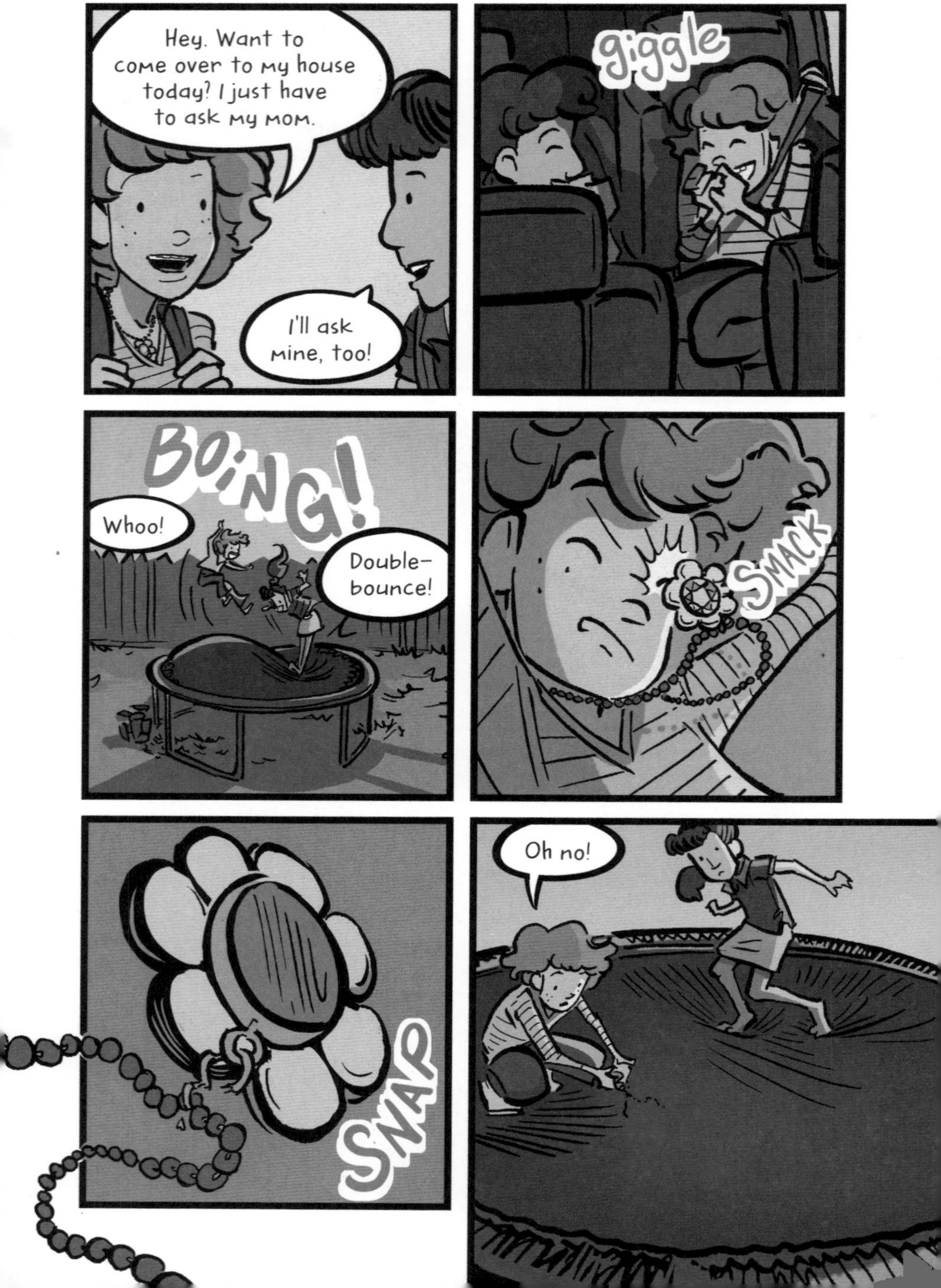
Hey. Want to come over to my house today? I just have to ask my mom.
I'll ask mine, too!
giggle
BOING!
Whoo!
Double-bounce!
SMACK
SNAP
Oh no!

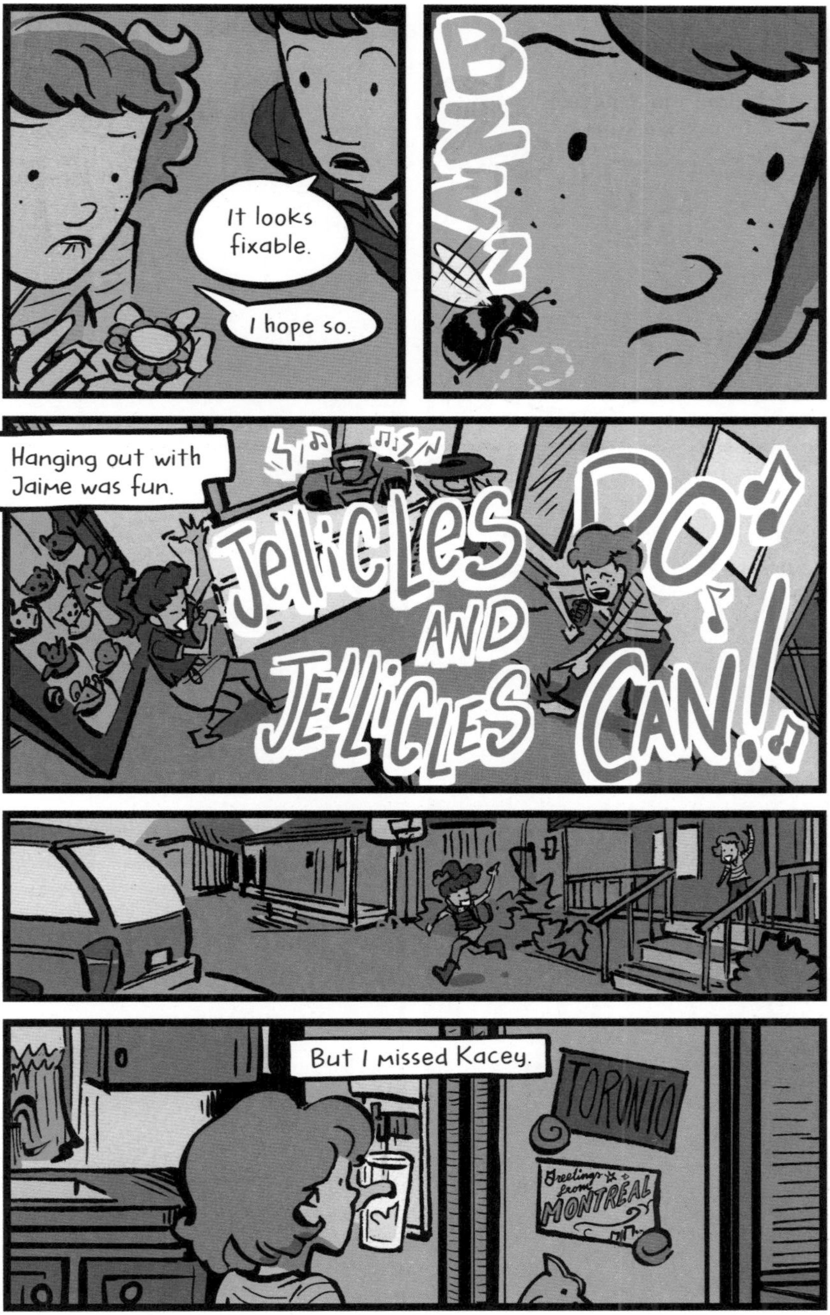
It looks fixable.
I hope so.
BZZZZ
Hanging out with Jaime was fun.
Jellicles DO AND Jellicles CAN!
But I missed Kacey.
TORONTO
Greetings from MONTREAL

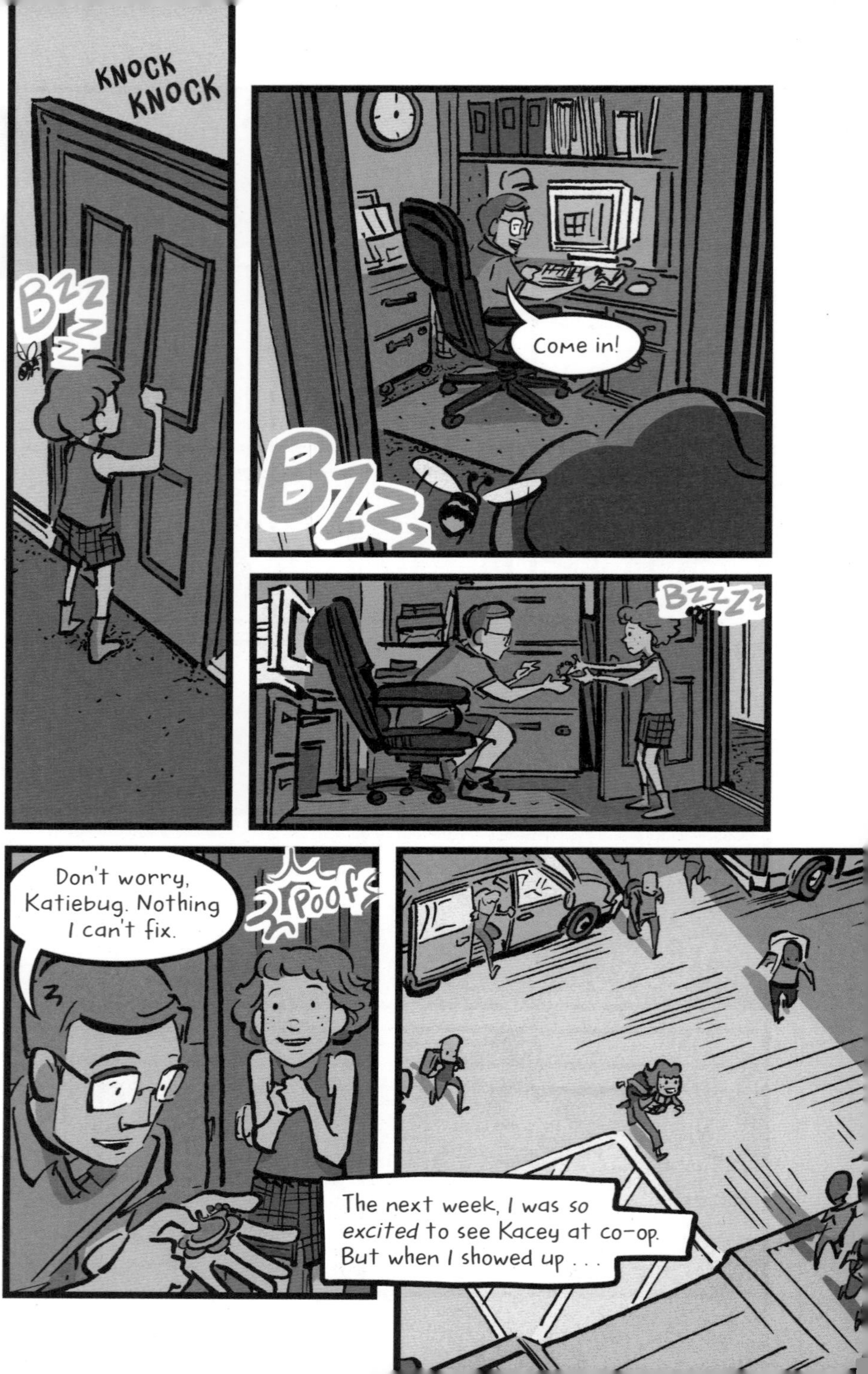
KNOCK KNOCK
BZZZZ
Come in!
BZZZ
BZZZZZ
Don't worry, Katiebug. Nothing I can't fix.
POOF
The next week, I was so *excited* to see Kacey at co-op. But when I showed up . . .

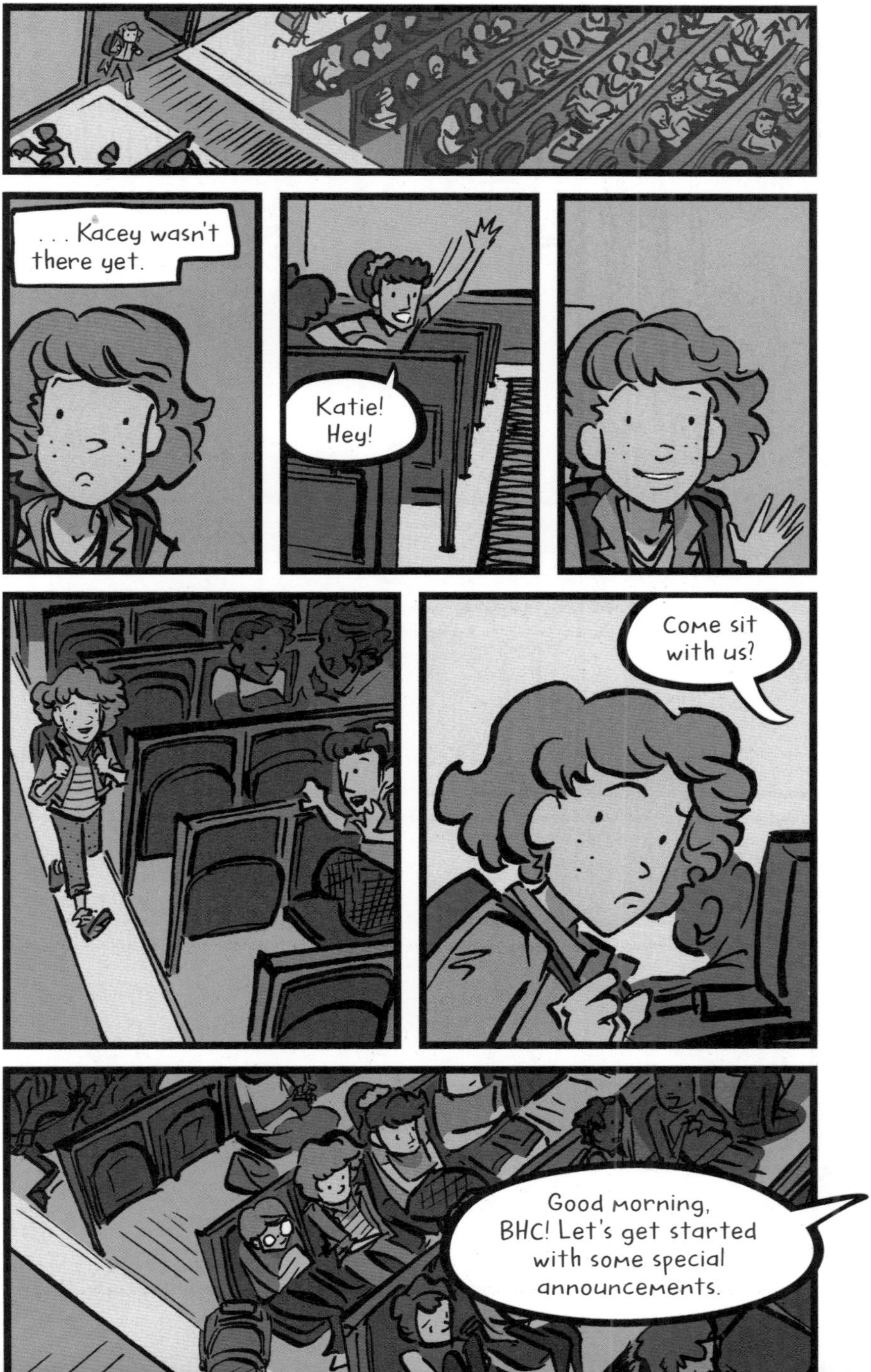
. . . Kacey wasn't there yet.
Katie! Hey!
Come sit with us?
Good morning, BHC! Let's get started with some special announcements.

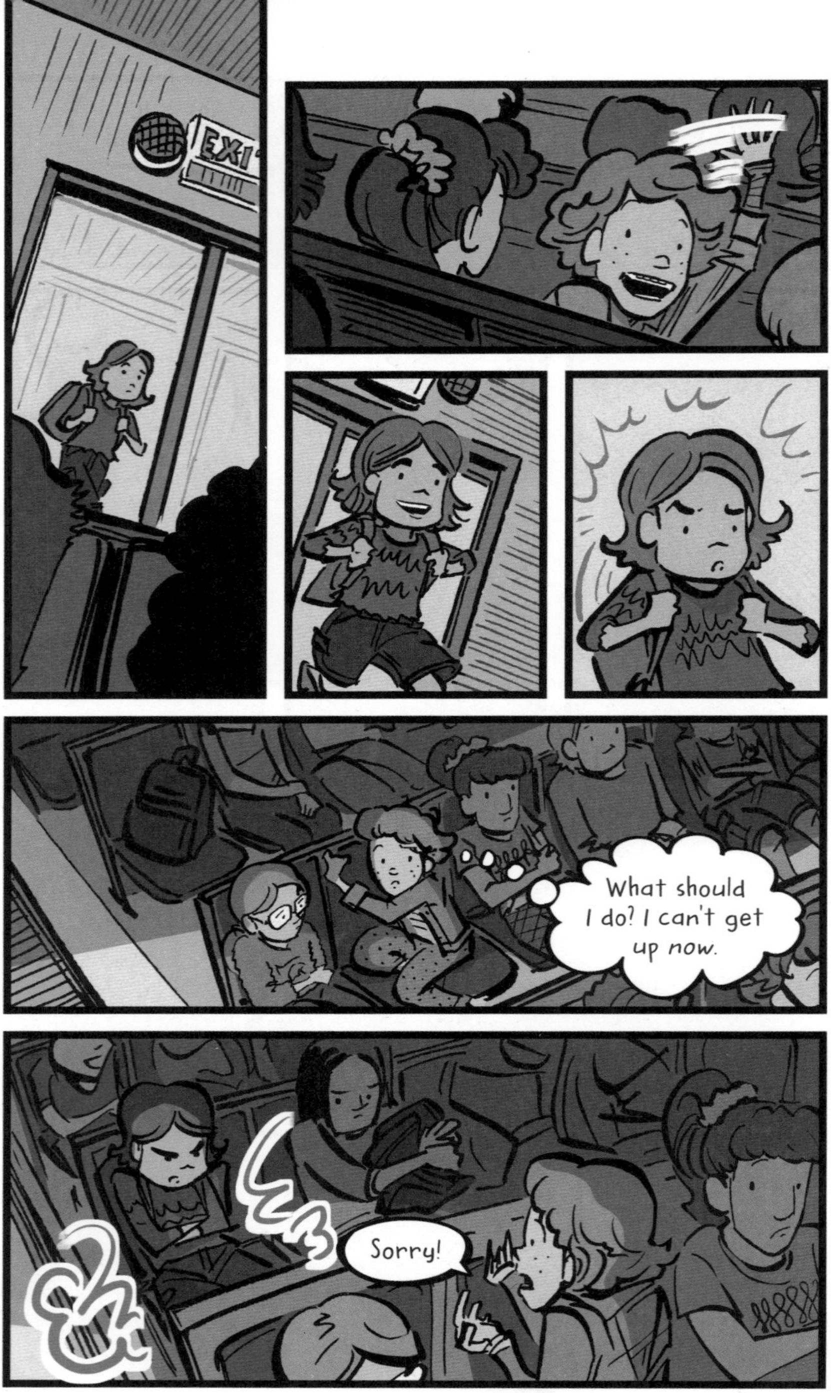

EXIT
What should I do? I can't get up now.
Sorry!

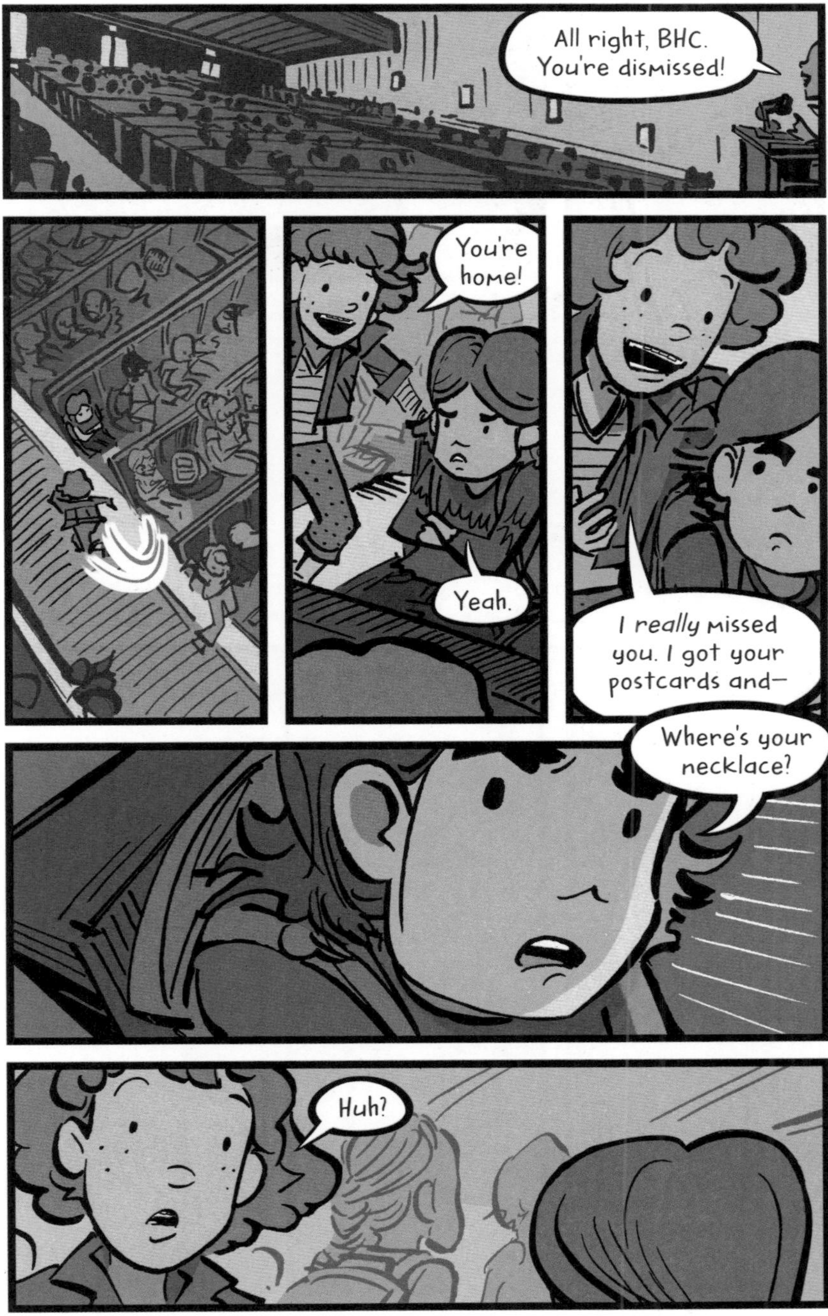
All right, BHC. You're dismissed!
You're home!
Yeah.
I *really* missed you. I got your postcards and—
Where's your necklace?
Huh?

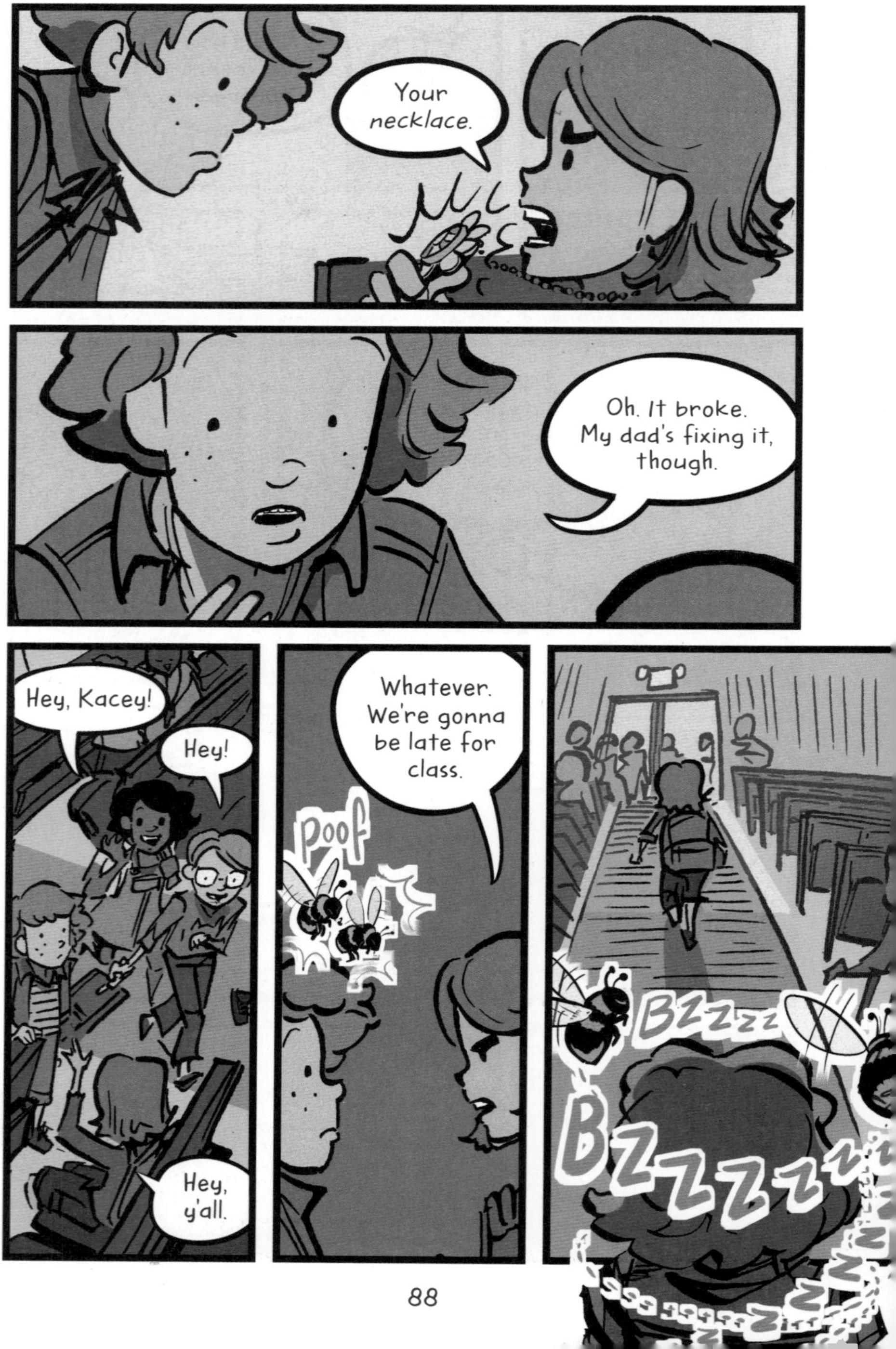

Your necklace.
Oh. It broke. My dad's fixing it, though.
Hey, Kacey!
Hey!
Hey, y'all.
Whatever. We're gonna be late for class.
poof
BZZzzz
BZZZZZZZZ

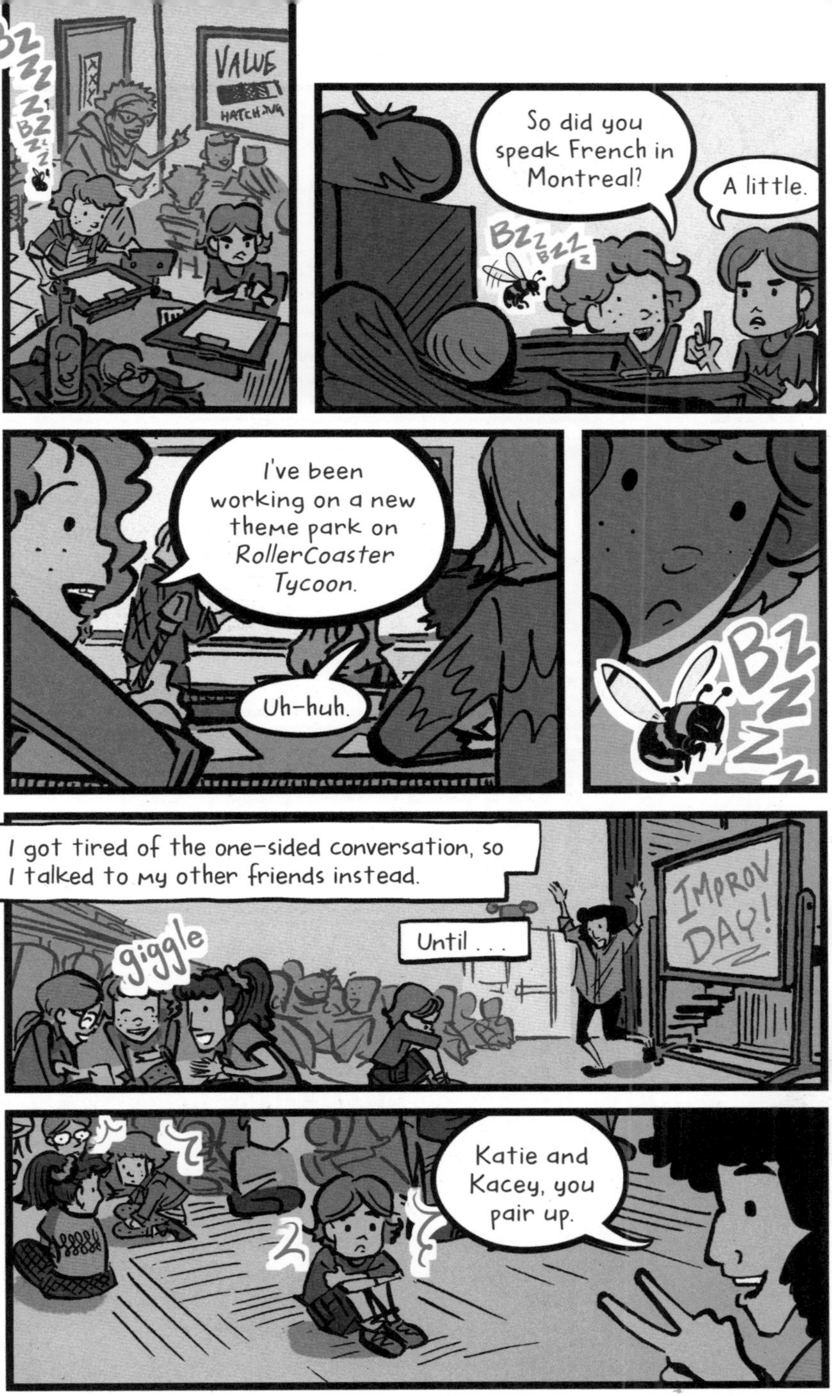

BZZZ
ZBZZZ
VALUE
So did you speak French in Montreal?
A little.
BZZZ BZZZ
I've been working on a new theme park on *RollerCoaster Tycoon.*
Uh-huh.
BZZZ
I got tired of the one-sided conversation, so I talked to my other friends instead.
giggle
Until . . .
IMPROV DAY!
Katie and Kacey, you pair up.

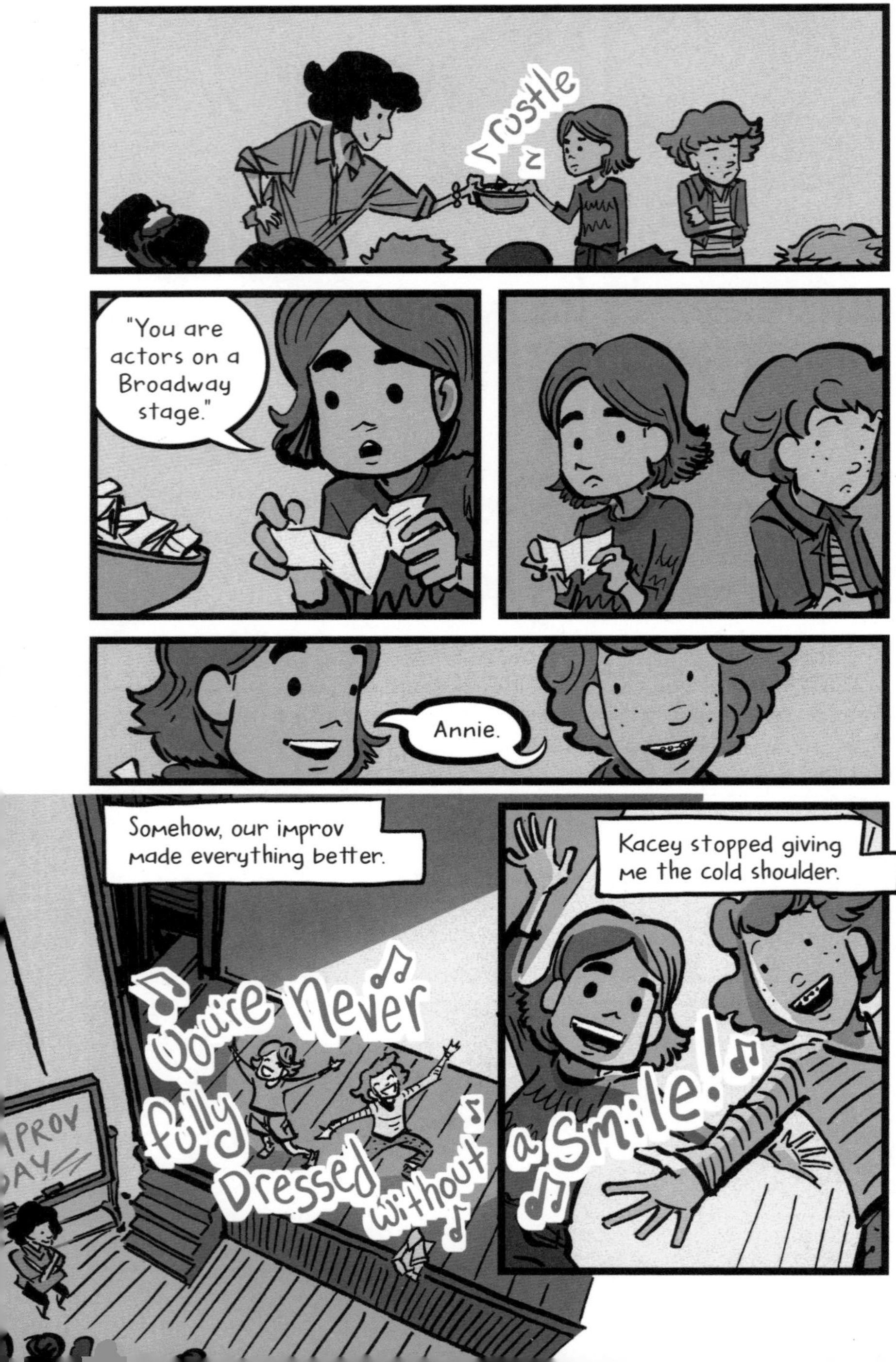

~rustle~
"You are actors on a Broadway stage."
Annie.
Somehow, our improv made everything better.
IMPROV DAY
Kacey stopped giving me the cold shoulder.
You're never fully dressed without a smile!

HA HA HA HA HA

Hey!

poof

That was so good, you two.

Thanks!

Kacey, this is Jaime.

Jaime, this is my best friend, Kacey.

Cool. Nice to meet you.

You too.

poof

Everything was back to normal, the way it had been before camp.

That day, I went over to Kacey's house.
I think we should include a reprise of "It's the Hard-Knock Life."
You mean "Hard *Not* Life"?

I'm pretty sure it's "Hard-Knock Life."

Like...

KNOCK

That doesn't make sense. What does "hard *knock*" even mean?

I dunno, it's just a saying.

What does "hard *not*" mean?

You know, like all the stuff the orphans aren't:

Not rich,

not loved,

not cared for.

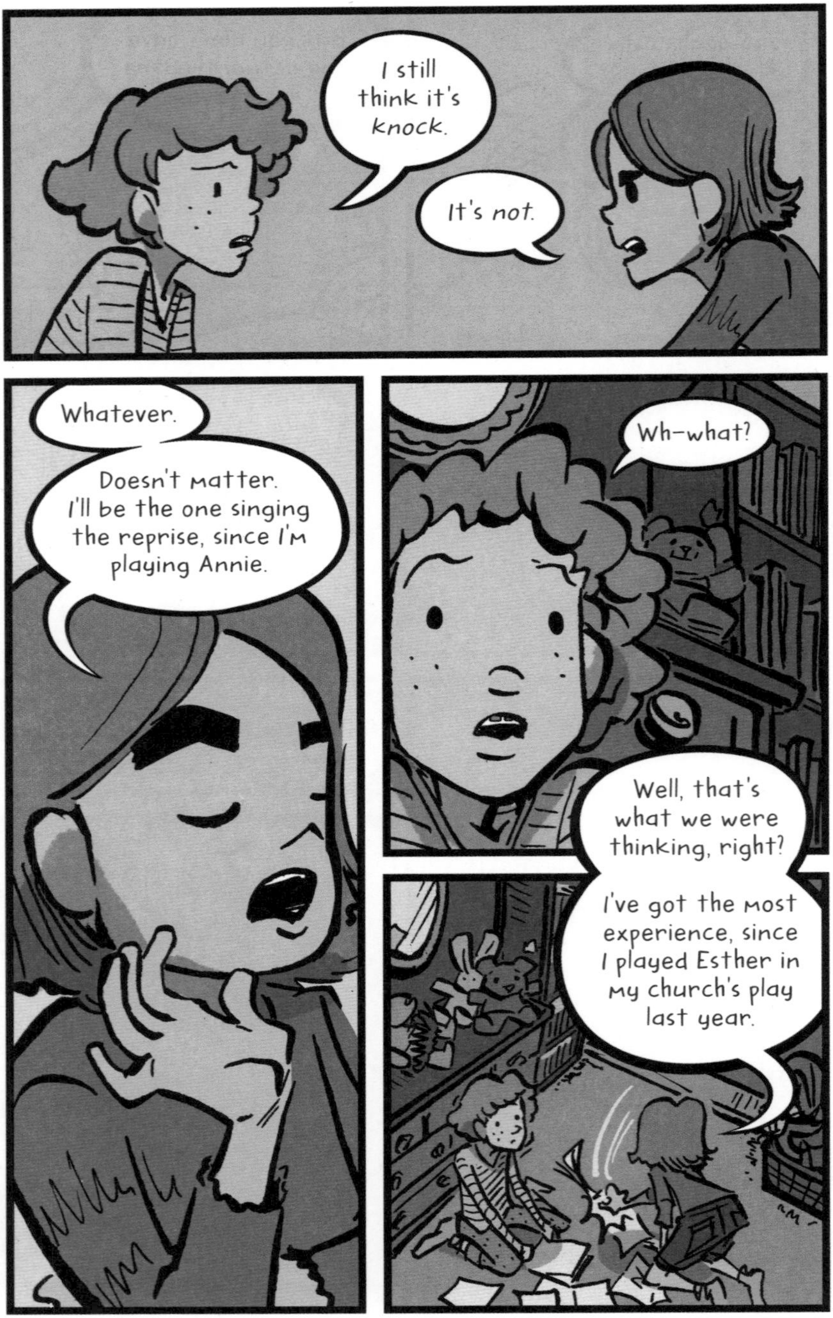
I still think it's *knock*.
It's *not*.
Whatever.
Doesn't matter. I'll be the one singing the reprise, since I'm playing Annie.
Wh-what?
Well, that's what we were thinking, right?
I've got the most experience, since I played Esther in my church's play last year.

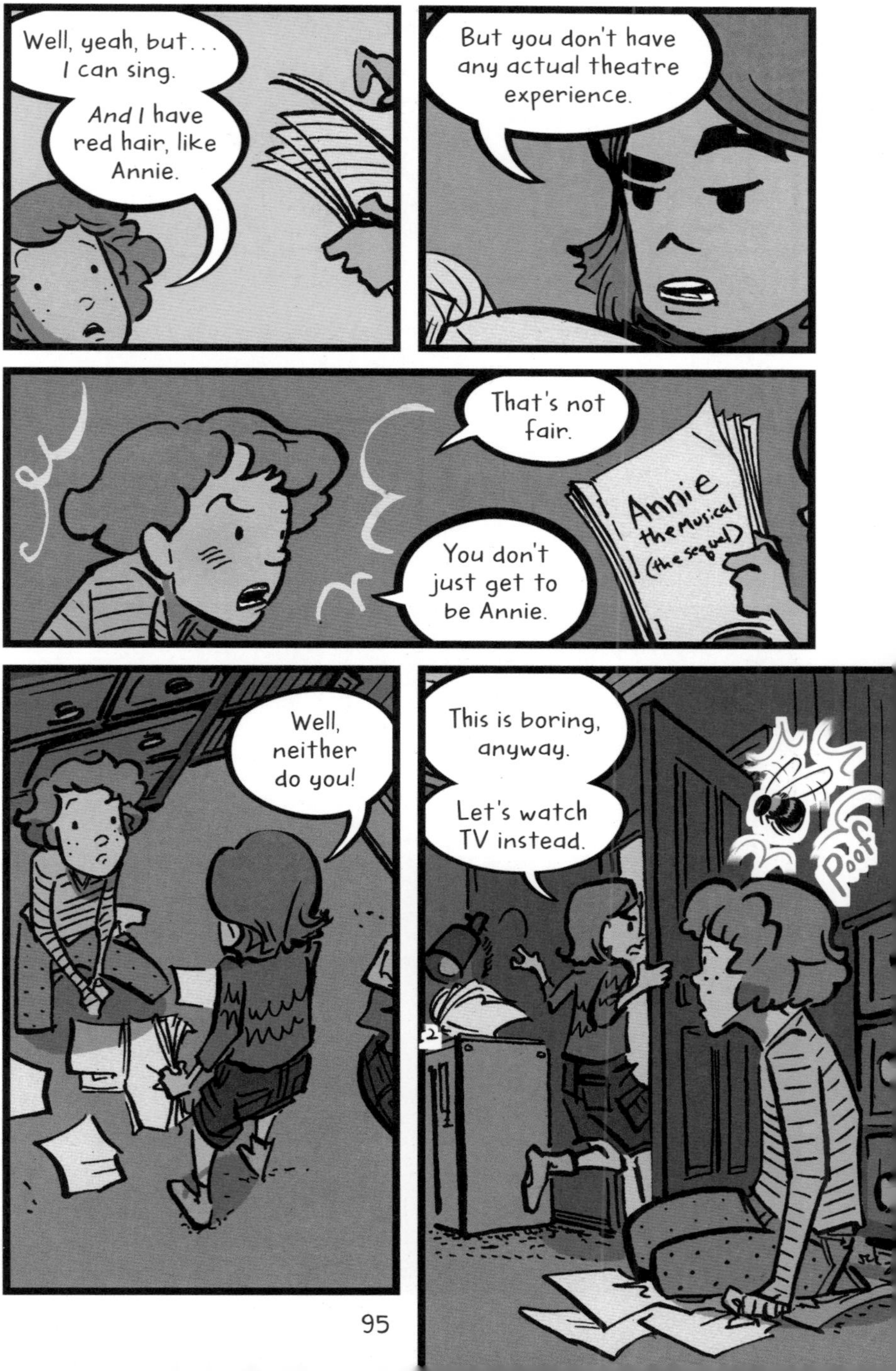
Well, yeah, but...
I can sing.
And I have red hair, like Annie.
But you don't have any actual theatre experience.
That's not fair.
You don't just get to be Annie.
Annie the Musical (the sequel)
Well, neither do you!
This is boring, anyway.
Let's watch TV instead.
Poof

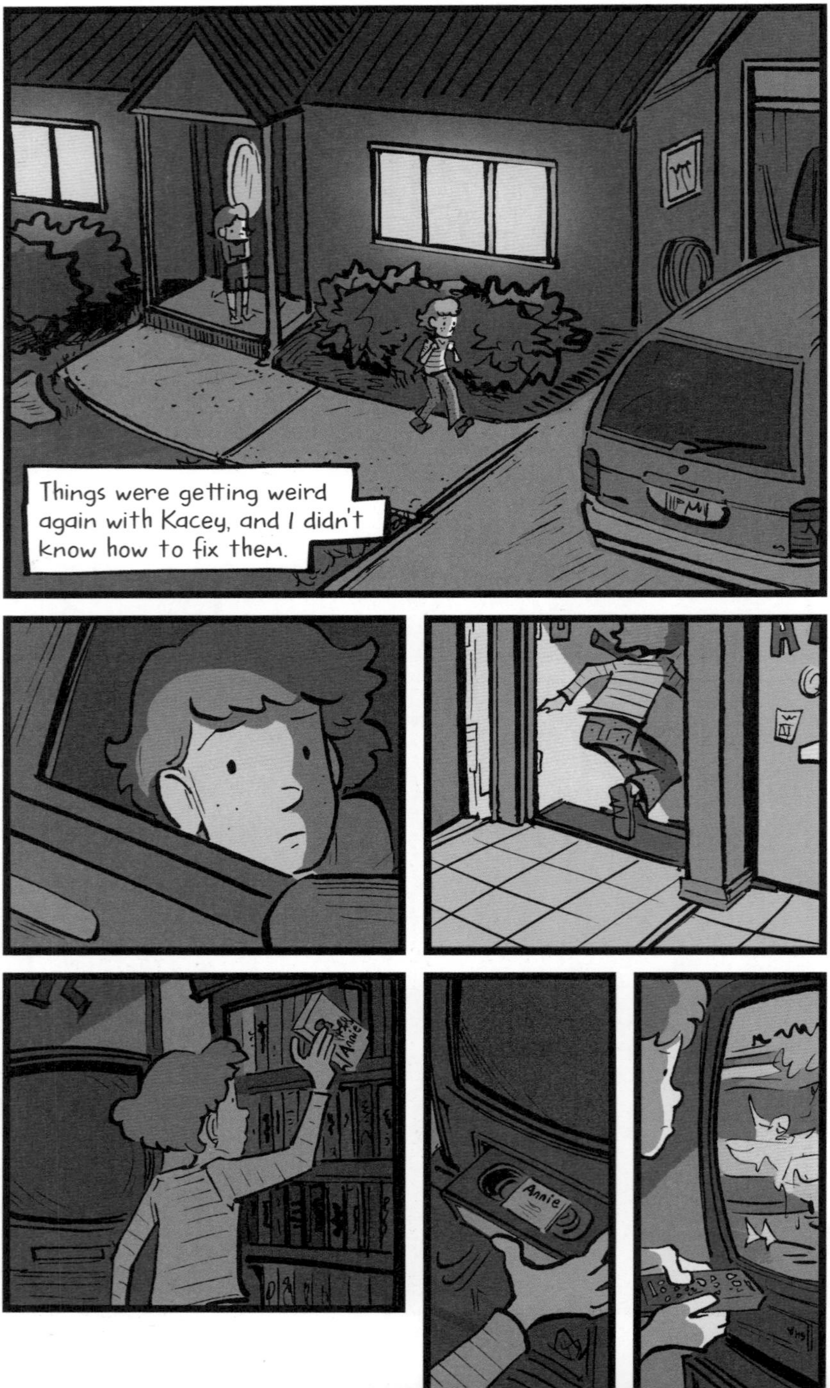
Things were getting weird again with Kacey, and I didn't know how to fix them.
Annie
Annie

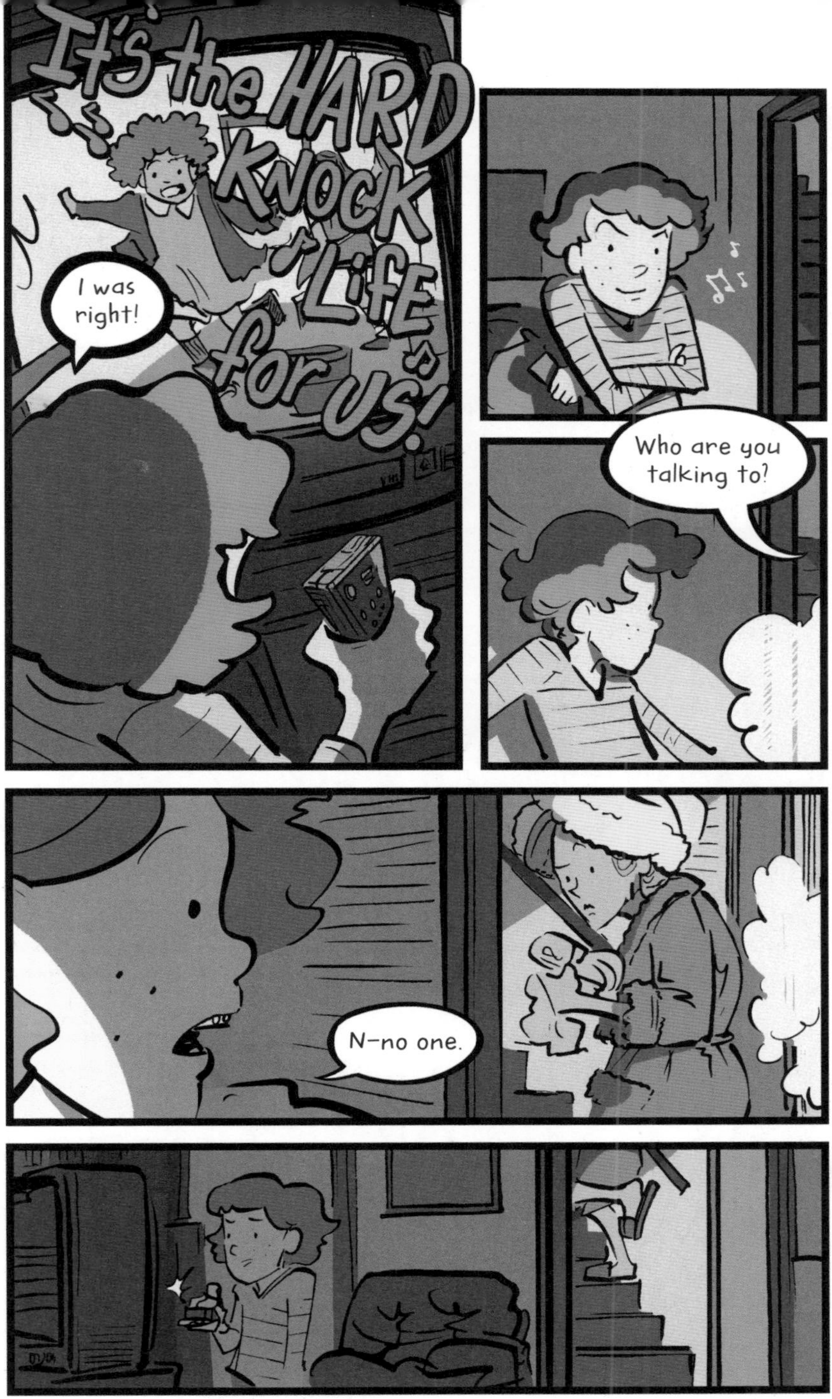
It's the HARD KNOCK LIFE for US!
I was right!
Who are you talking to?
N-no one.

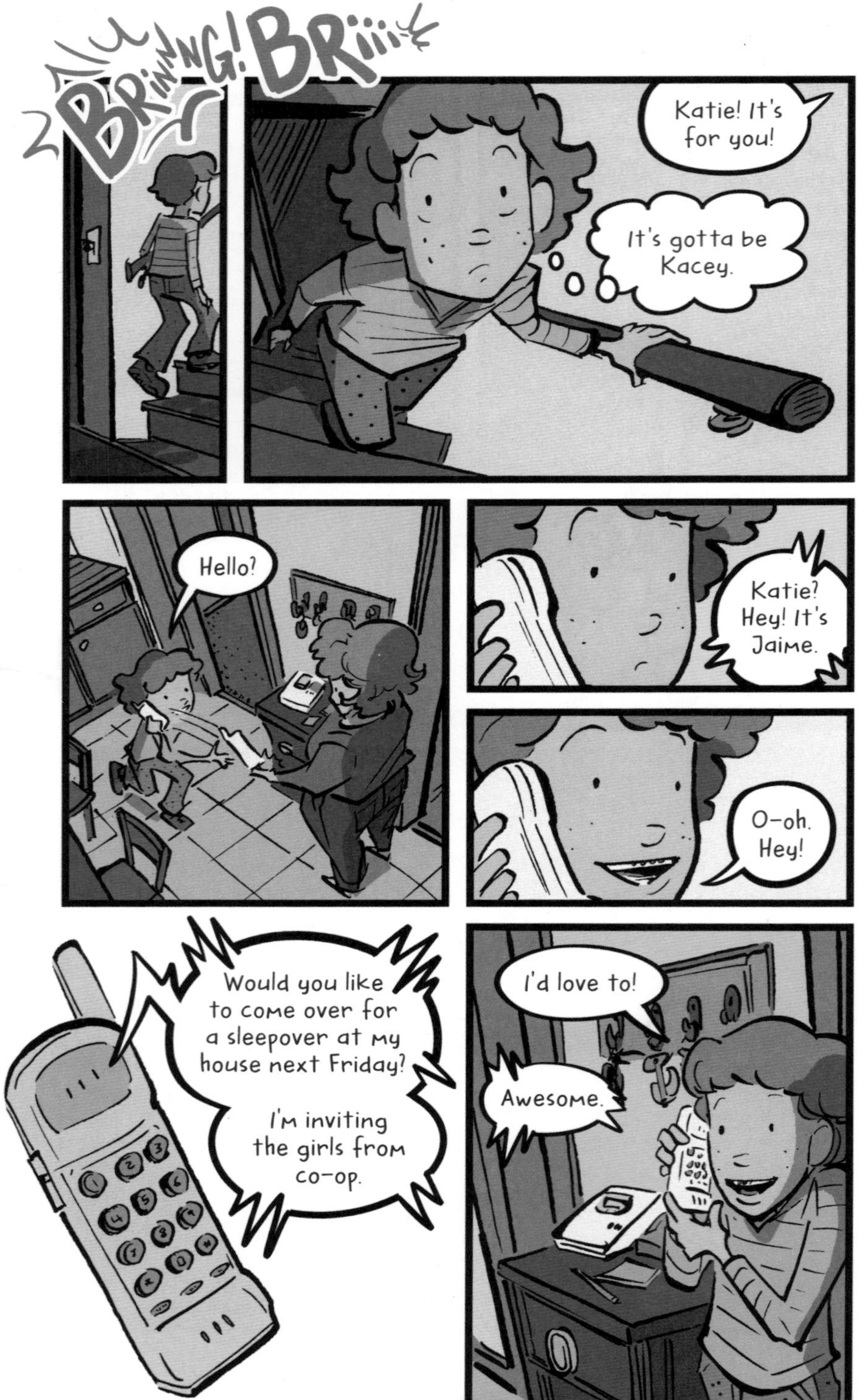

BRiNNNG! BRiiii
Katie! It's for you!
It's gotta be Kacey.
Hello?
Katie? Hey! It's Jaime.
O-oh. Hey!
Would you like to come over for a sleepover at my house next Friday?
I'm inviting the girls from co-op.
I'd love to!
Awesome.

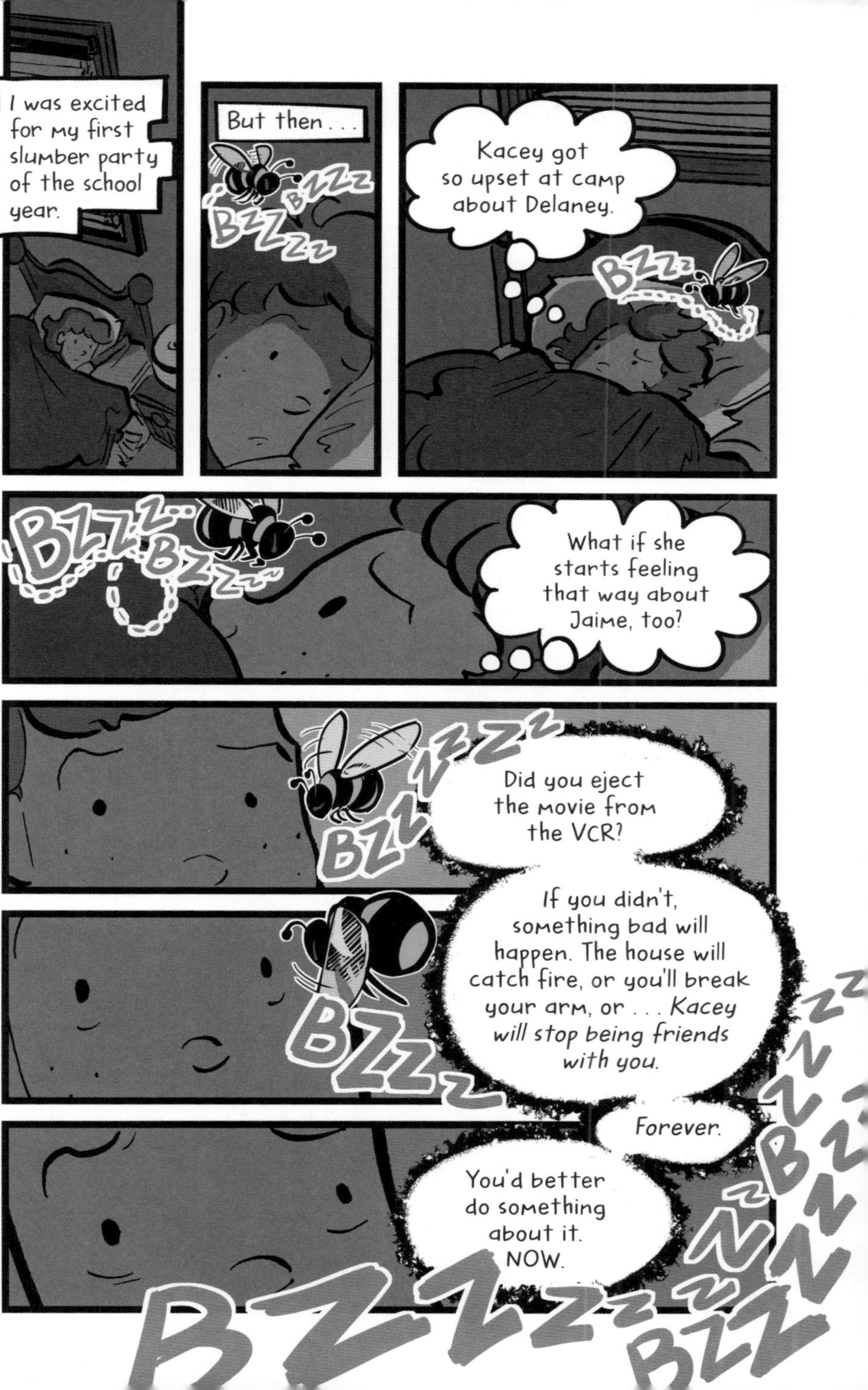

I was excited for my first slumber party of the school year.
But then . . .
BZZZ BZZZZ
Kacey got so upset at camp about Delaney.
BZZZ
BZZZ.. BZZZ
What if she starts feeling that way about Jaime, too?
BZZZZZ
Did you eject the movie from the VCR?
If you didn't, something bad will happen. The house will catch fire, or you'll break your arm, or . . . Kacey will stop being friends with you.
BZZZ
Forever.
You'd better do something about it. NOW.
BZZZZZ
BZZZZZ

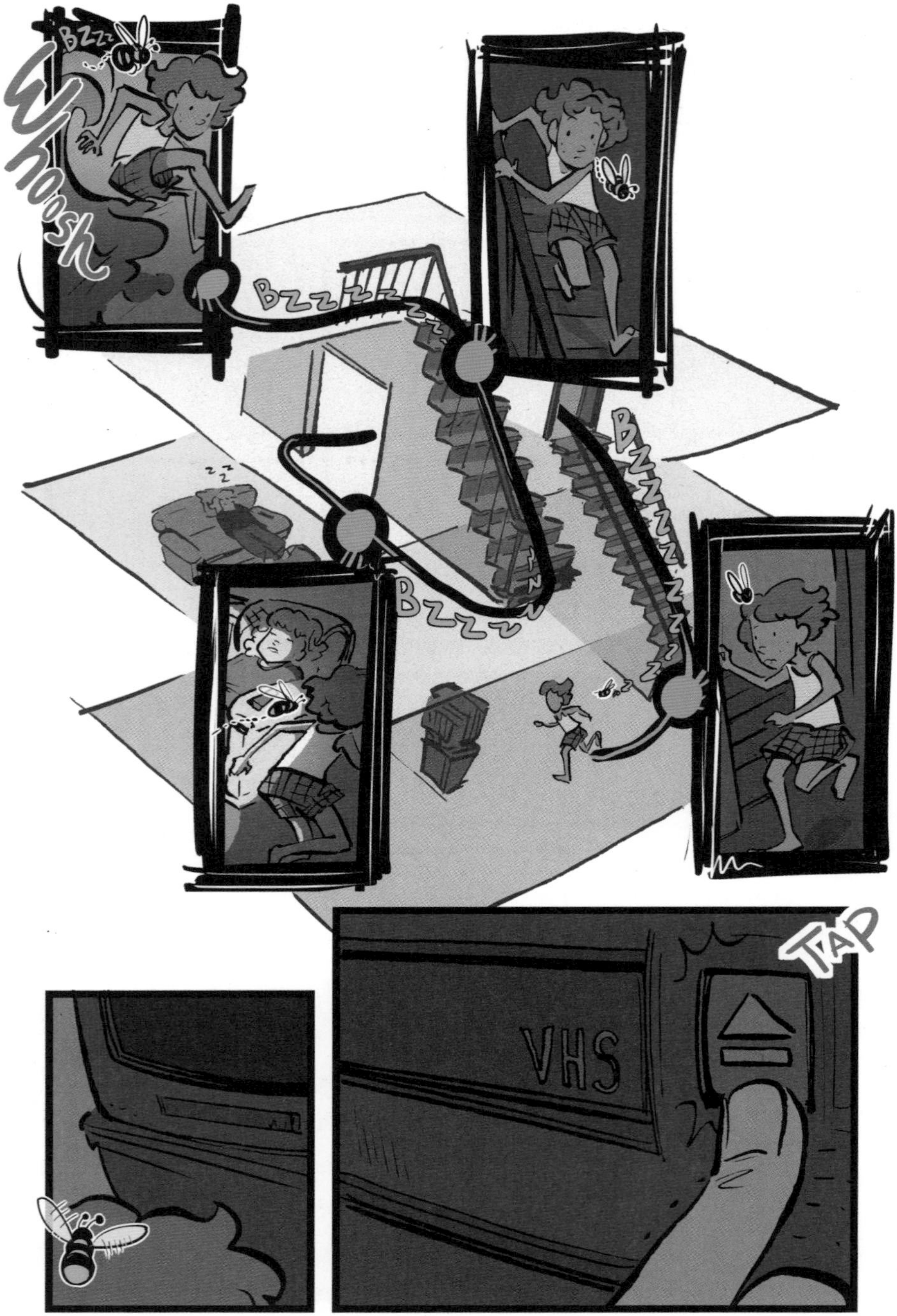
Whoosh
TAP
VHS

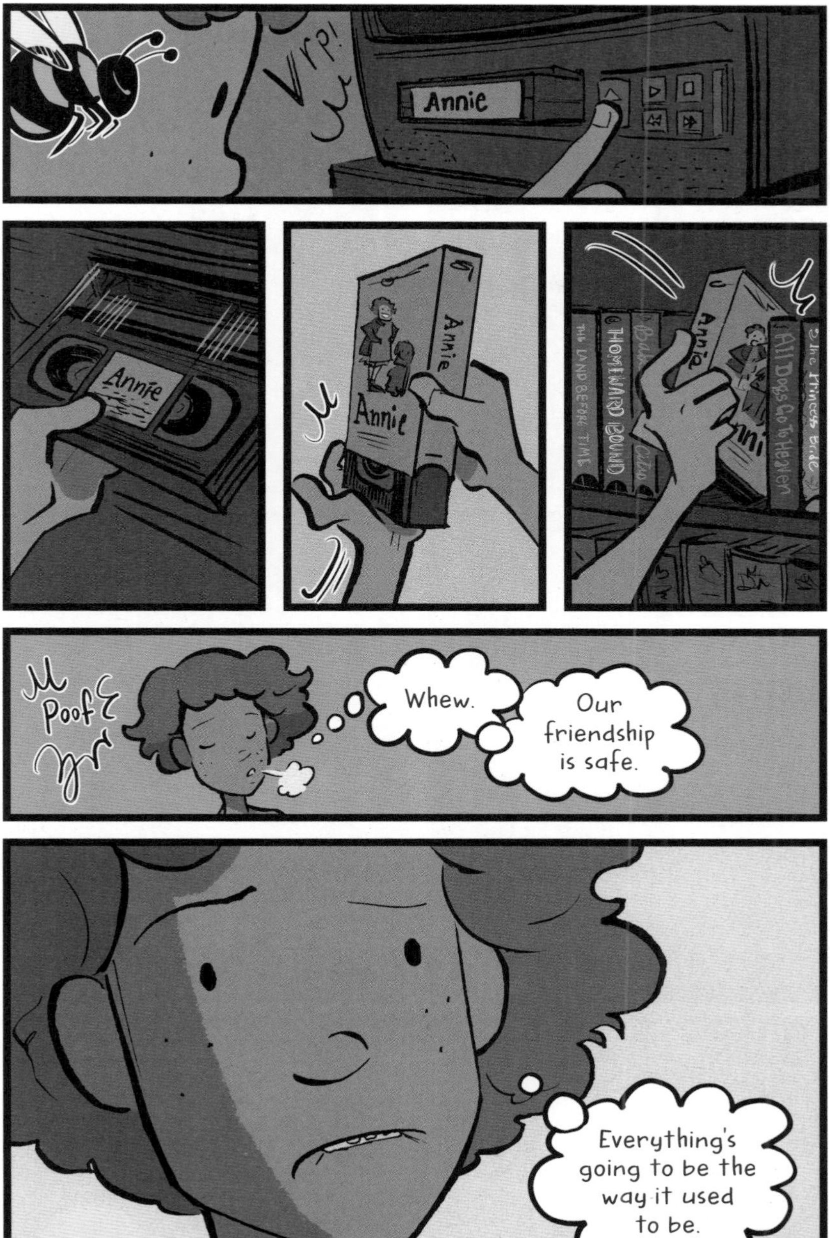
Vrp!
Annie
Annie
Annie
Annie
Annie
The Land Before Time
Homeward Bound
All Dogs Go to Heaven
The Princess Bride
Poof
Whew.
Our friendship is safe.
Everything's going to be the way it used to be.

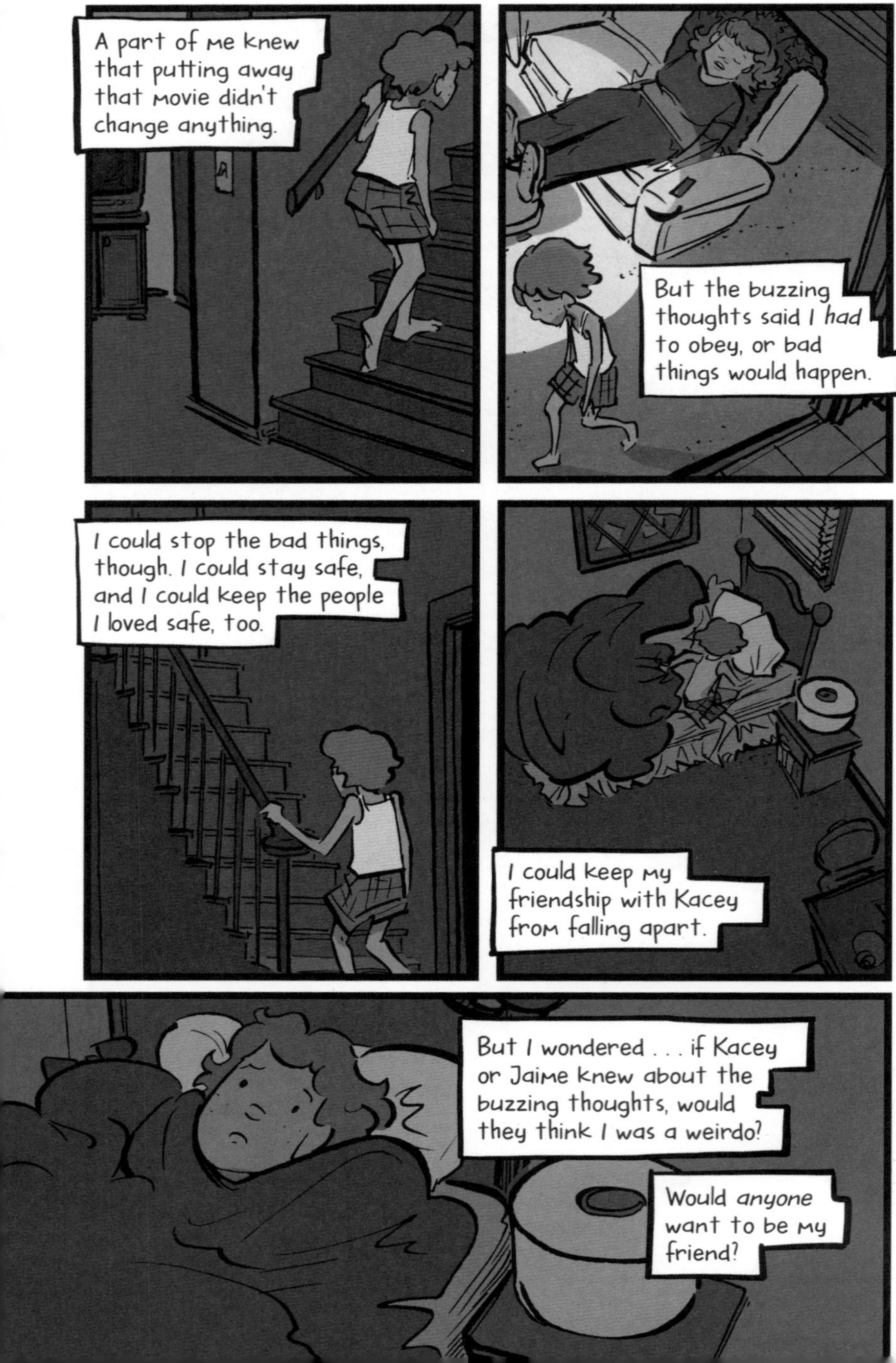
A part of me knew that putting away that movie didn't change anything.
But the buzzing thoughts said I *had* to obey, or bad things would happen.
I could stop the bad things, though. I could stay safe, and I could keep the people I loved safe, too.
I could keep my friendship with Kacey from falling apart.
But I wondered . . . if Kacey or Jaime knew about the buzzing thoughts, would they think I was a weirdo?
Would *anyone* want to be my friend?

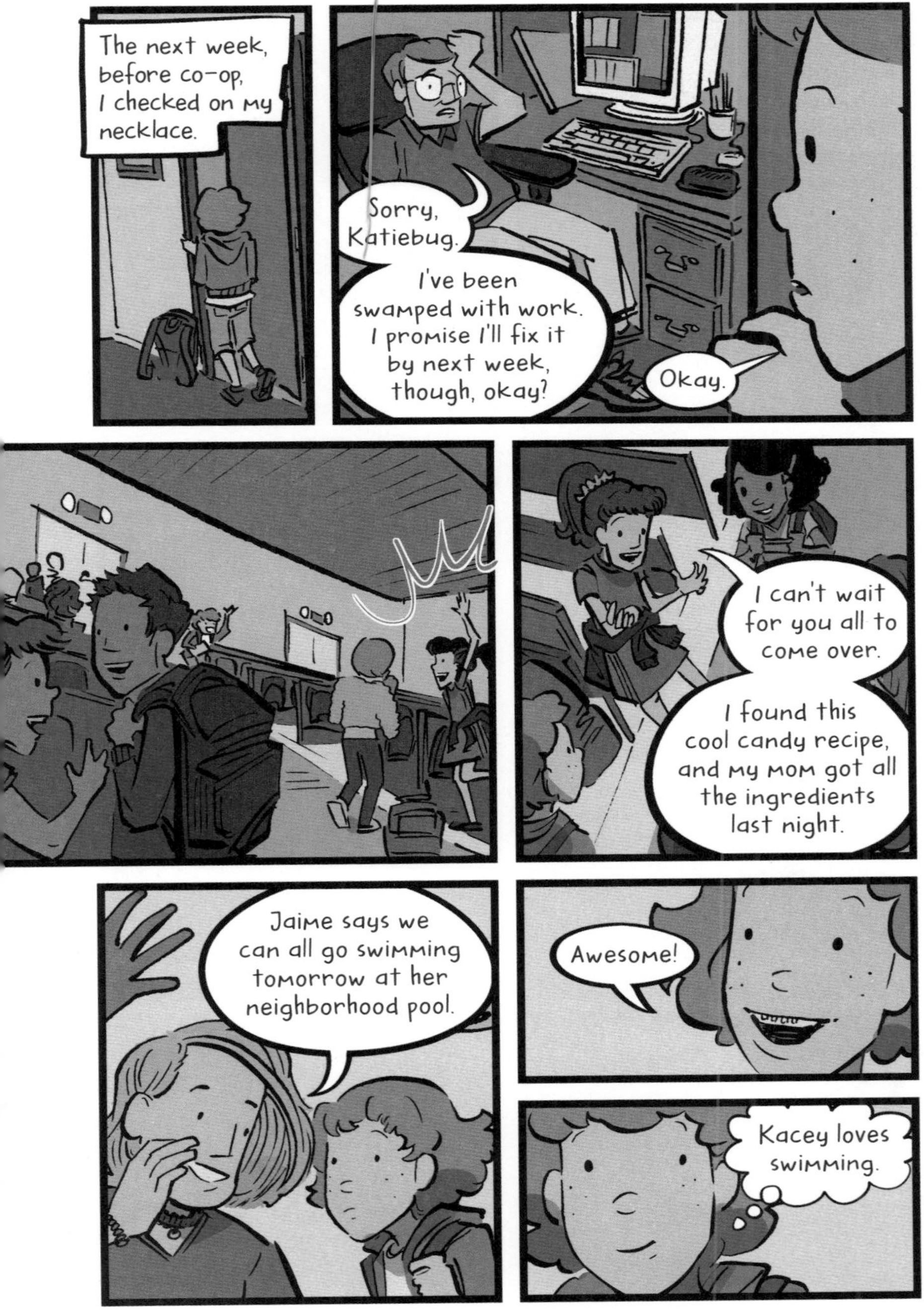

The next week, before co-op, I checked on my necklace.
Sorry, Katiebug.
I've been swamped with work. I promise I'll fix it by next week, though, okay?
Okay.
I can't wait for you all to come over.
I found this cool candy recipe, and my mom got all the ingredients last night.
Jaime says we can all go swimming tomorrow at her neighborhood pool.
Awesome!
Kacey loves swimming.

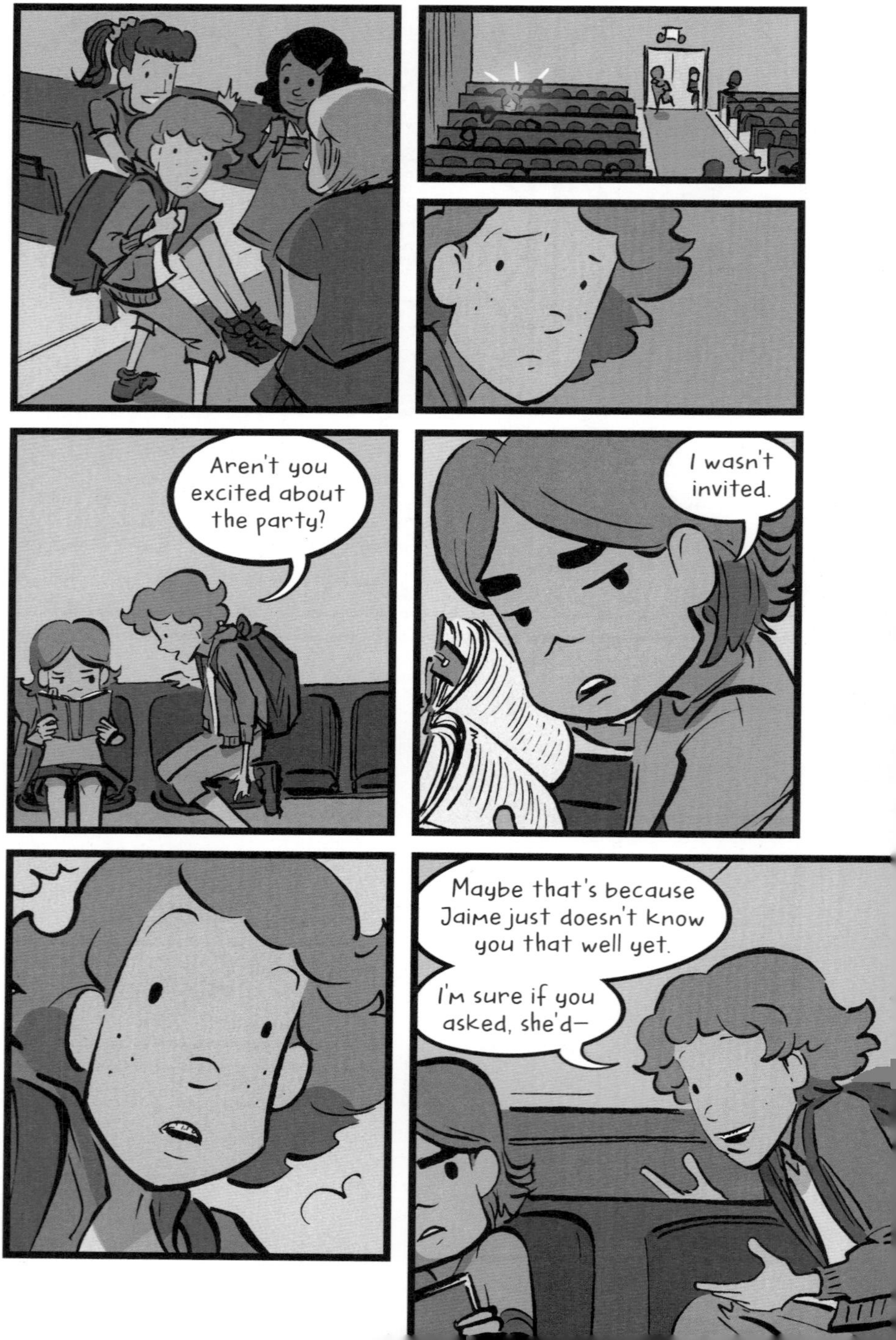
Aren't you excited about the party?
I wasn't invited.
Maybe that's because Jaime just doesn't know you that well yet.
I'm sure if you asked, she'd—

I'm not going to *invite myself* to some random girl's party.

I'm sorry. When Kacey said the co-op girls were going, I thought—

If you're really my best friend, you won't go.

What?

I guess you like your new friends more than me.

Pop!

But Lauren, Megan, and Callie—they're your friends, too.

Not anymore. They're obsessed with, like, makeup and shopping.

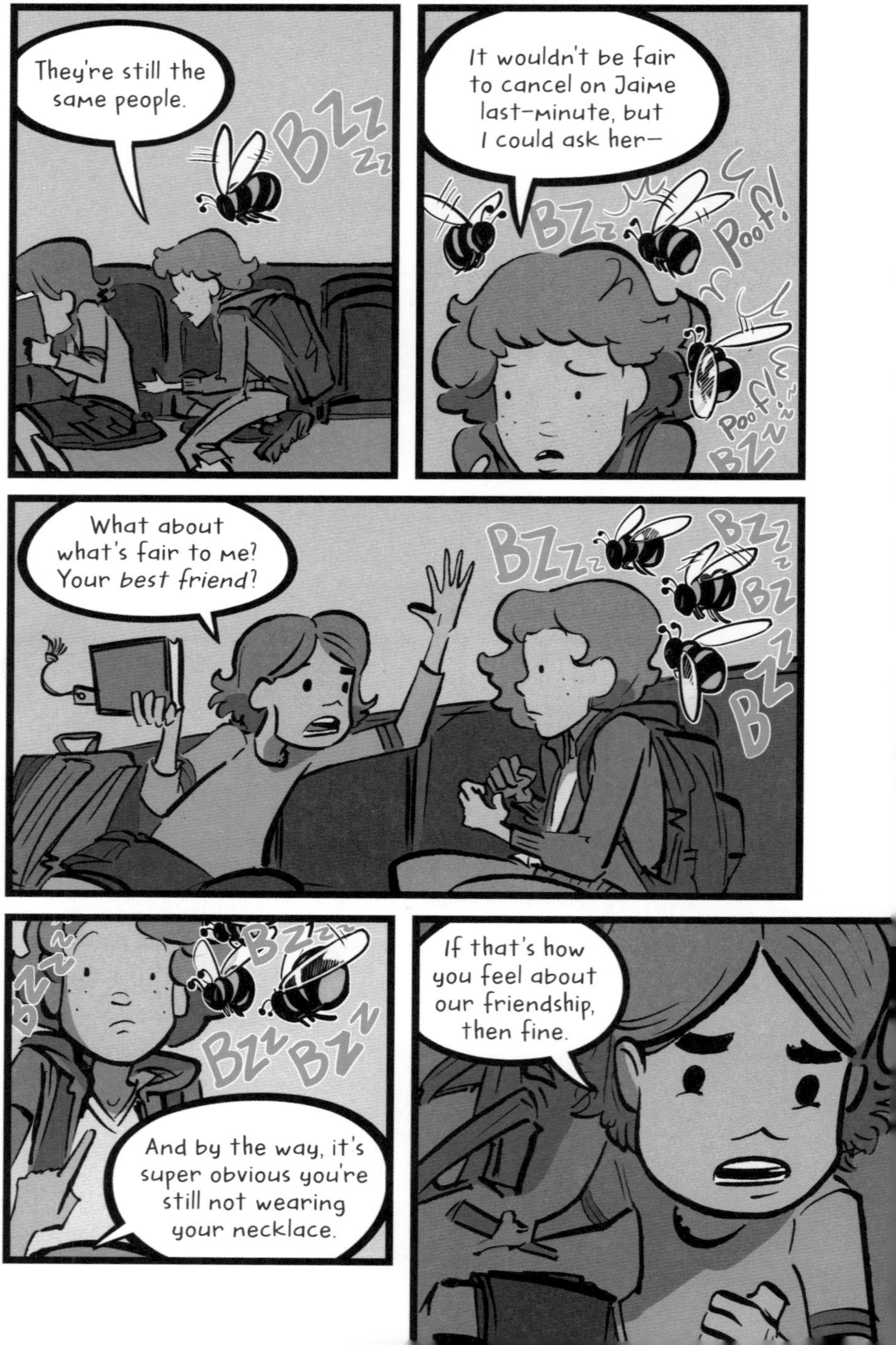
They're still the same people.
BZZ zz
It wouldn't be fair to cancel on Jaime last-minute, but I could ask her—
BZZ
Poof!
Poof!
BZZ
What about what's fair to me? Your *best friend*?
BZZZ
BZZ
BZ
BZ
BZZ
BZZ
BZZ
If that's how you feel about our friendship, then fine.
And by the way, it's super obvious you're still not wearing your necklace.

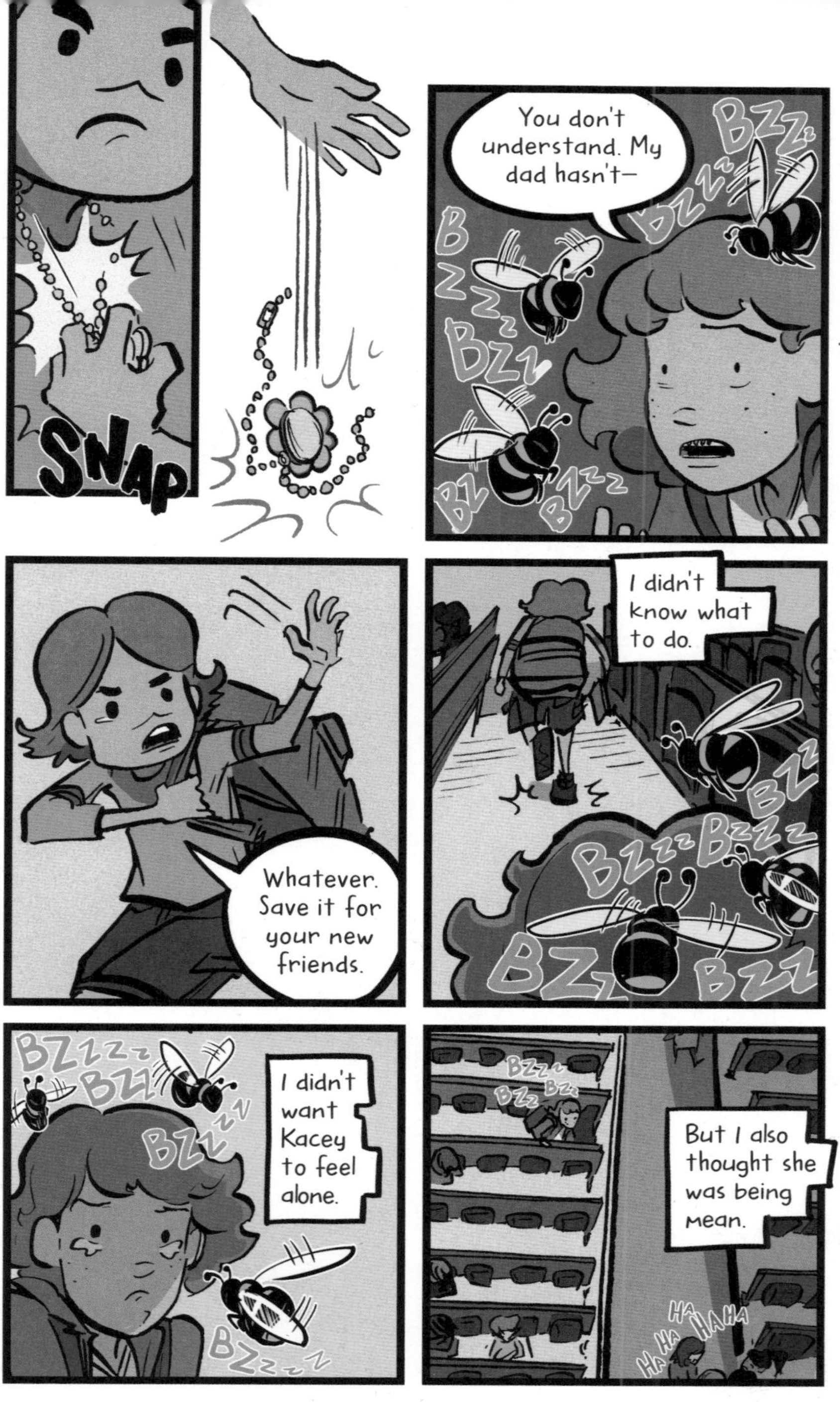
SNAP
You don't understand. My dad hasn't—
BZZZ
Whatever. Save it for your new friends.
I didn't know what to do.
BZZZ
I didn't want Kacey to feel alone.
BZZZ
But I also thought she was being mean.
HA HA HA HA HA HA

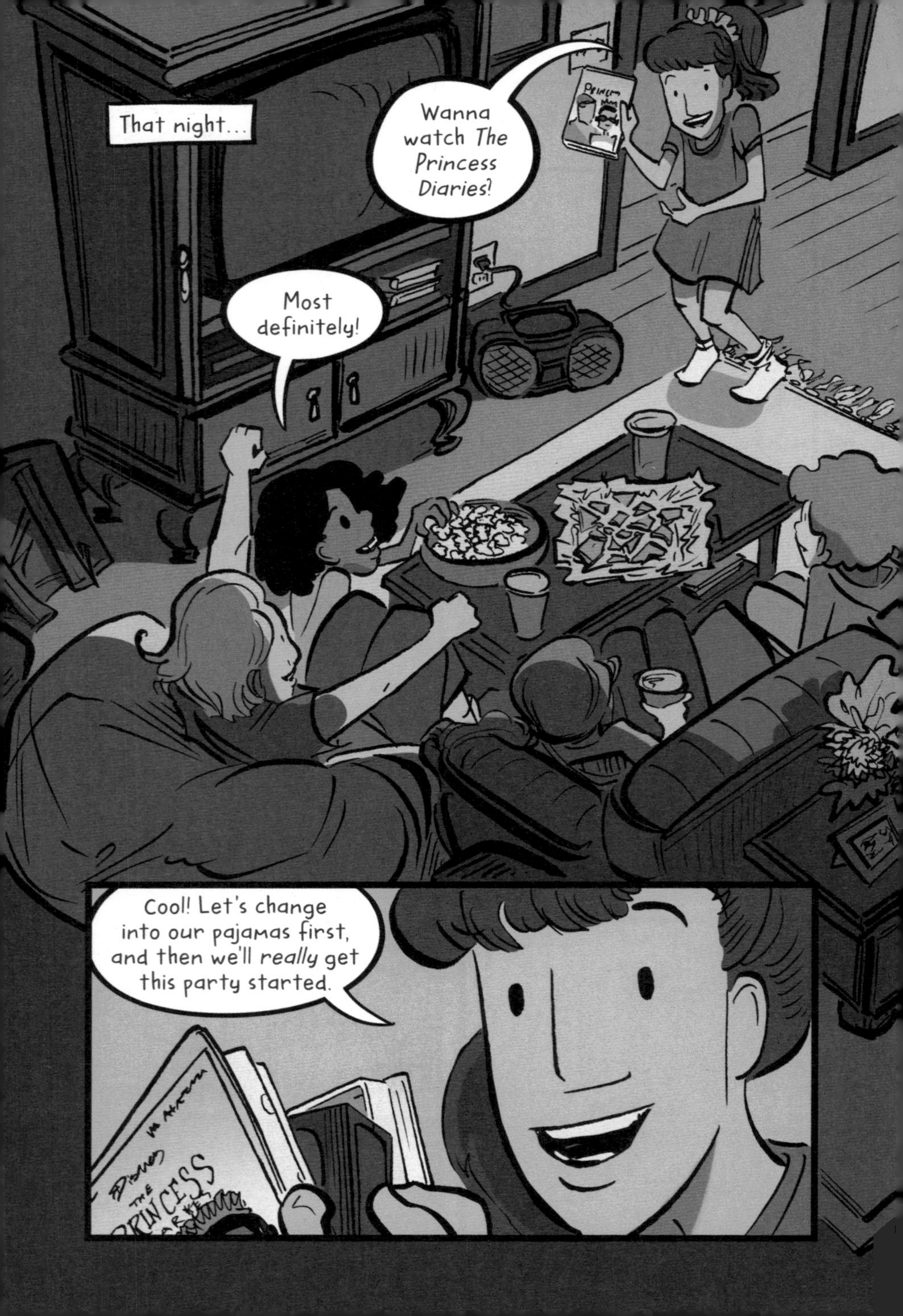
That night...
Wanna watch *The Princess Diaries*?
Most definitely!
Cool! Let's change into our pajamas first, and then we'll *really* get this party started.

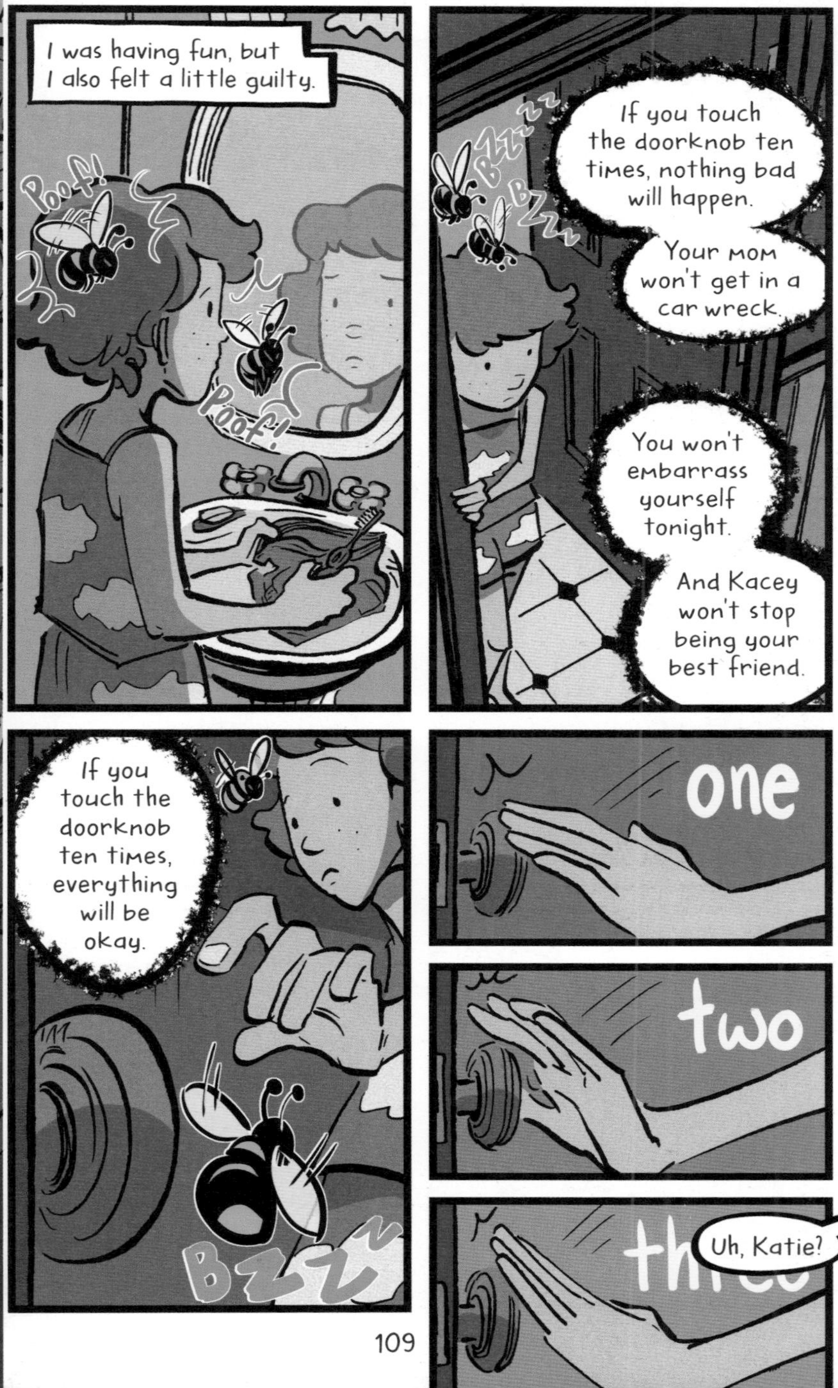
I was having fun, but I also felt a little guilty.
Poof!
Poof!
BZZzzz
BZzz
If you touch the doorknob ten times, nothing bad will happen.
Your mom won't get in a car wreck.
You won't embarrass yourself tonight.
And Kacey won't stop being your best friend.
If you touch the doorknob ten times, everything will be okay.
BZZZ
one
two
Uh, Katie?

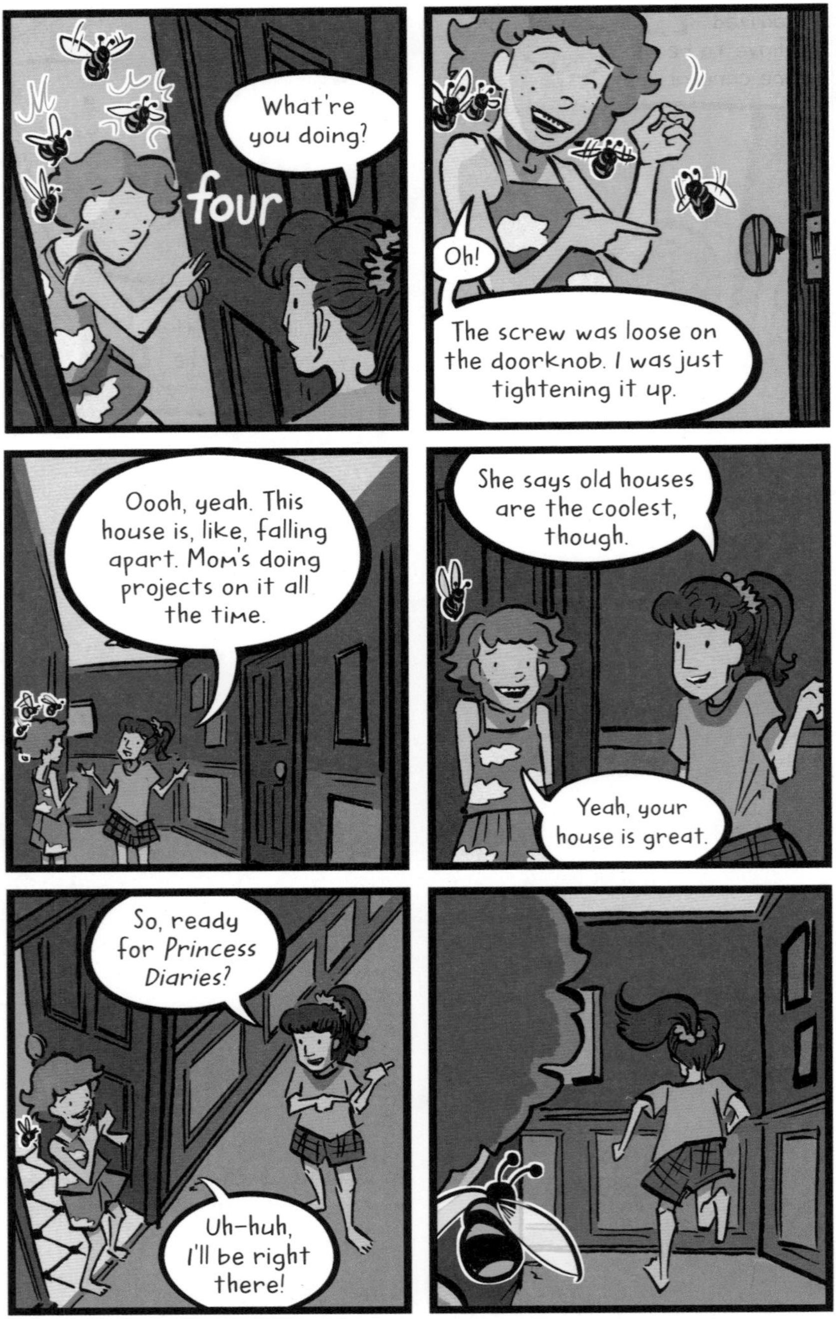

four
What're you doing?
Oh!
The screw was loose on the doorknob. I was just tightening it up.
Oooh, yeah. This house is, like, falling apart. Mom's doing projects on it all the time.
She says old houses are the coolest, though.
Yeah, your house is great.
So, ready for *Princess Diaries*?
Uh-huh, I'll be right there!

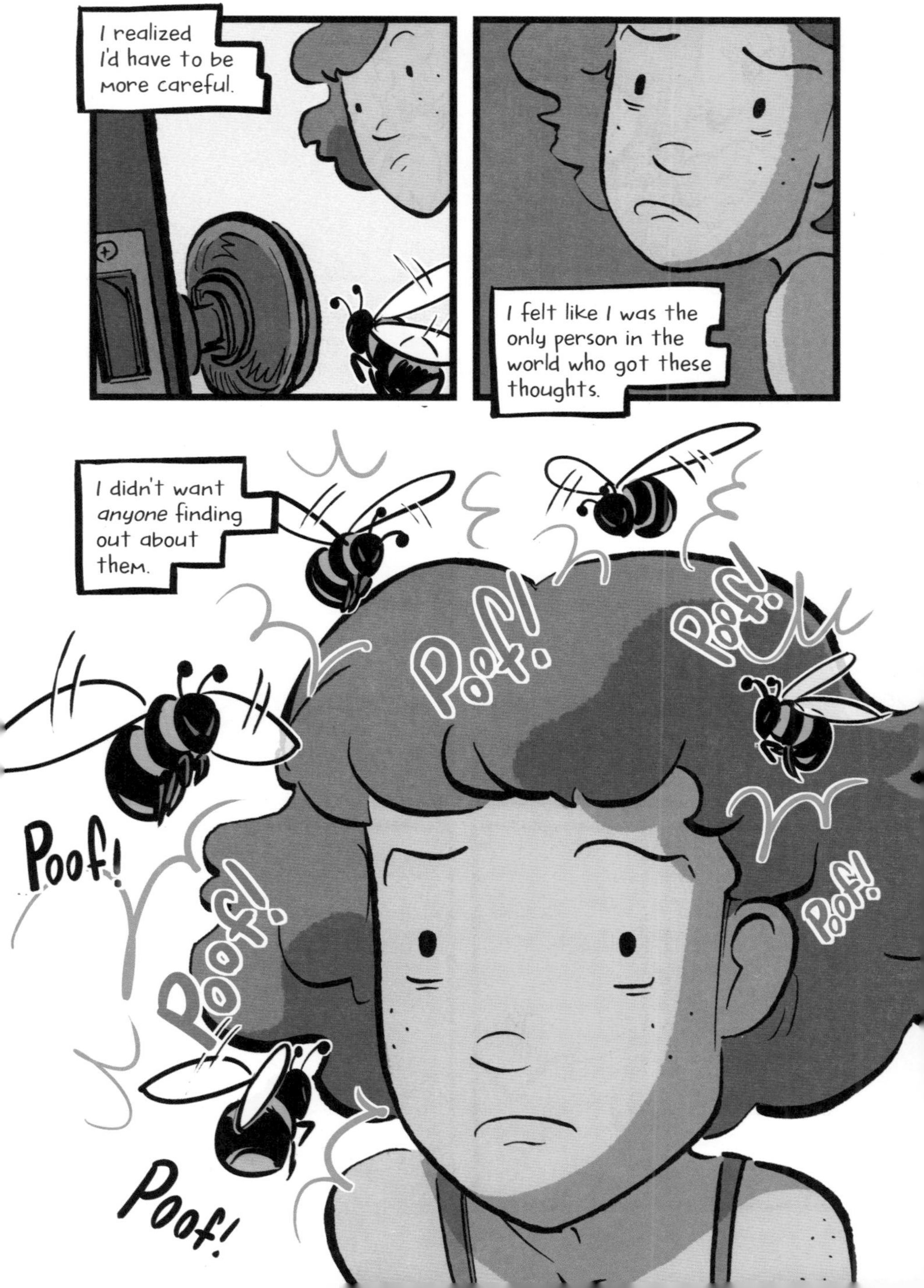
I realized I'd have to be more careful.
I felt like I was the only person in the world who got these thoughts.
I didn't want *anyone* finding out about them.
Poof!
Poof!
Poof!
Poof!
Poof!
Poof!

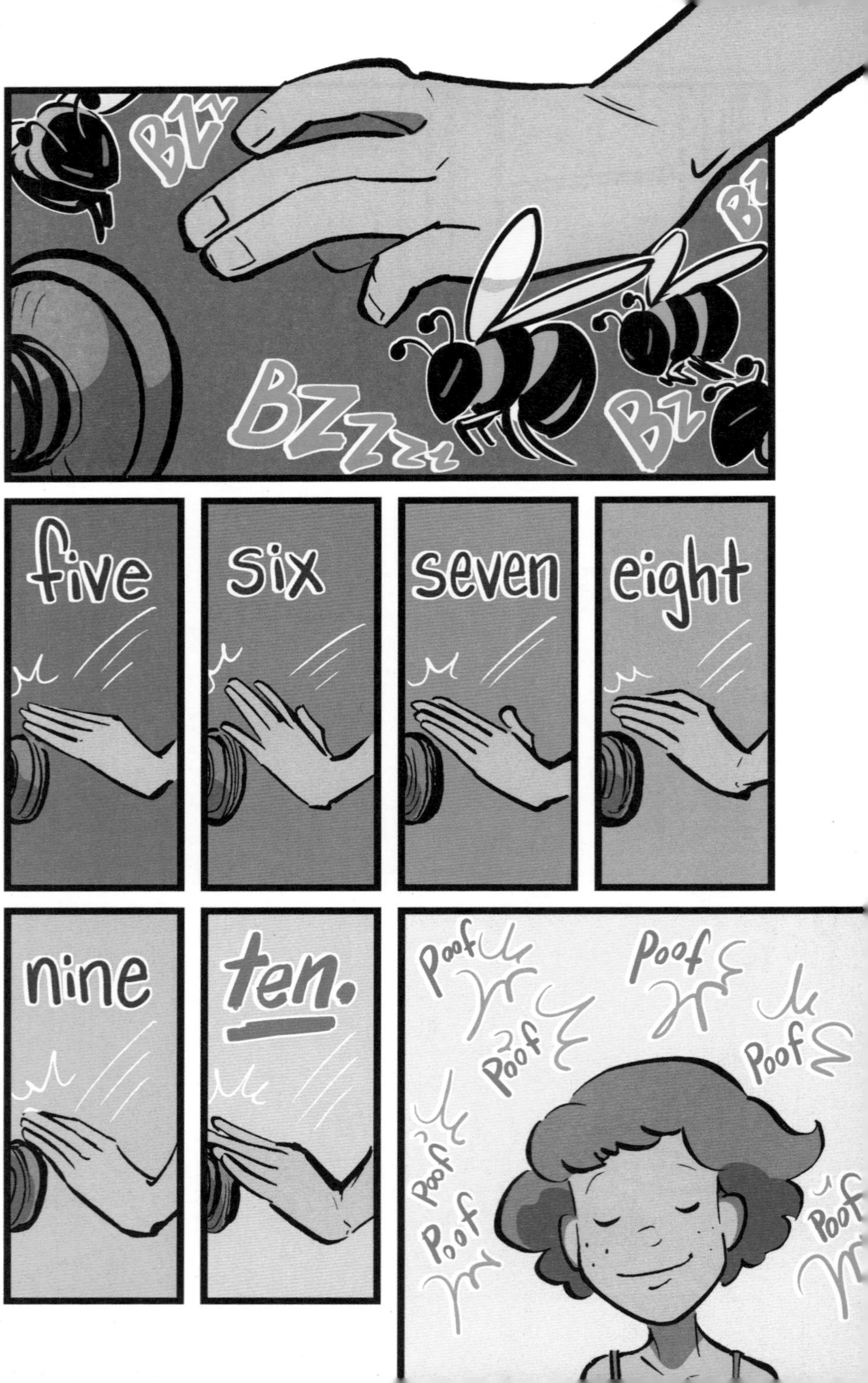

BZZ
BZ
BZZZZZ
BZ
five
six
seven
eight
nine
ten.
Poof
Poof
Poof
Poof
Poof
Poof
Poof
Poof

I didn't hear from Kacey all week.

I thought about calling her.

But . . .

. . . maybe she didn't want to be friends anymore.

Jaime, Lauren, Callie, and Megan were still my friends.

HA HA HA HA HA HA HA HA HA HA HAHA

I missed Kacey, though.

Dear America
KNOCK KNOCK
Hey, Katiebug! I fixed it.
Oh. Thanks.
Everything okay?
Yeah, I'm fine.
CLICK

I got you set up for your dentist appointment in December.

Dr. Kramer will be able to tell us if you need that surgery.

But I probably won't, right?

Poof!

Well, I don't know. We'll see.

BZzzzz

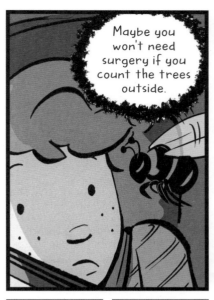

Maybe you won't need surgery if you count the trees outside.

 one
 two

 three
 four

 five
 six

 seven  eight
 nine  ten

Yeah.

I won't need surgery.

Poof!

I tried to focus on fun stuff, like drama class.

Katie and Jaime, why don't you come up here and show us your skit?

WOO!
CLAP
CLAP
CLAP
WHOO!
CLAP
YAY!
YEAH!
CLAP
CLAP
CLAP
CLAP
CLAP
CLAP
WOO!
We got a standing ovation.
That's great.
Hey! Take a look at this.
"Fayette County Children's Theatre . . ."
FAYETTE COUNTY
CHILDREN'S THEATRE
OPEN AUDITIONS
The Adventures of Madeline

". . . open auditions for *The Adventures of Madeline*."

I know how much you love drama class. Would you be interested in auditioning for a play?

YES!

A professional theatrical production?

It was a dream come true.

And way more impressive than some play at co-op or church.

Wait till I get cast.

Then who will have *actual theatre experience!*

The next week . . .
CHILDREN'S THEATRE
Whoa.
This place is so cool.
I feel like I'm in New York City.
LDREN'S THEATRE

Hey there!

Do you have a résumé and headshot?

SIGN IN

RÉSUMÉ

I hope it's not weird that my headshot is a Christmas portrait.

POOF!

We'll be taking you upstairs, where you'll receive the scenes we'd like you to perform.
SIGN IN
Please take time to study them as you wait.
Break a leg!
EXIT

I was nervous. But mostly? I was excited.

Next up, we'd like to see Katie Ormsbee reading for Madeline!

I love to stretch!

And climb.

And rhyme!

Very nice, Katie.

Thank you.

He said *very* nice.

A few days later . . .

We would like to see the following young actors this Monday night . . .

Kevin Lee,

Jenny Nash,

Katie Ormsbee . . .

YES!!!

I have to tell Kacey. She won't believe—

Oh.

How'd I forget?

Poof!

CLick

BZZzz

We're not talking.

Callbacks were like auditions, only with fewer people.
And this time we were on an actual stage.
EXIT
Waiting for the cast list seemed to take *ages*.
EXERCISES IN LOGIC AND RHETORIC
But I tried to distract myself.
Tick tick
BHC ANNUAL HARVEST FESTIVAL

Poof!

Bzzz
Bzzz

Bzz *Bzz* *Bzz* *Bzz* *Bzz* *Bzz* *Bzz*

There were days when, if I was busy enough with other stuff, I could push the buzzing thoughts away.

BZzzz

But most of the time they felt like an itch I *had* to scratch.

BZzzz BZzz BZz BZz BZz BZzz BZ BZzz

The house won't burn down if you touch the cushion three times.

Turn on the faucet ten times.

Quick.

No one can know. If people find out, I won't have any friends.

BZzz BZzz BZzz

128

At last, the big day arrived.

Bzzz BEEP Beep Beep Beep Beep

For audition announcements, dial extension 317.

Beep Beep Beep

We're pleased to offer the following roles to our auditionees:

Madeline to Layla McKay . . .

Bzzz Zzz Bzz

I didn't get it.

. . . Pepito to Mark Bellos, Genevieve to Heather Chen, Miss Clavel to . . .

. . . Puppy #3 to Katie Ormsbee . . .

Bzz

Wait. I got a part?

Poof!

I got a part!
Sure, I'd be playing one of Genevieve's *twelve* puppies.
But I'd be performing at the opera house, where the children's theatre put on their holiday season play.
I was going to be in a real stage production.
I DID IT!
MOM! DAD! GUESS WHAT!

There'll be public performances on the weekend *and* school performances during the week.

It's going to be so official!

Congrats. That's pretty cool.

I was Puppy #3 this time, but in a couple of years? I'd be a star.

CLAP CLAP CLAP CLAP CLAP CLAP CLAP CLAP

MAD.
CAST→

AAH! HA HA WHERMUST
HA HA

Hey! Welcome to Team Genevieve!

I'm Sam.

I'm Alyssa, Puppy #2.

And I'm Jasmine, Puppy #4.

I'm right between you two!

It's weird, because we don't have any lines, right? But we still have to be here for blocking.

Blocking?

It's when they tell you where to go onstage.

I hear we're going to get puppy training.

Like, how to howl and bark and move like a dog.

Oh, I'm already good at that.

OW!

giggle

giggle

SHHH!

I can't wait to see the costumes.

Yeah, I wonder what our stage makeup will be like.

Have you all been in plays here before?
I haven't.
Don't worry. We'll stick together.
And we *did*. All four of us. Together, we aced our puppy training.
AWOOOOOo!
Woof Woof
Ruff!
Whiine
Break time!

SODA
Oh my God, you all. The new Harry Potter book.
I'm only midway through. Don't spoil it!
Do you pronounce his name *Sed*-ric or *Ked*-ric Diggory?
I can't believe we have to wait *so long* till the next one!
I had tons of fun hanging out with Team Genevieve. No one even thought that my being homeschooled was weird.
Hey, we're theatre nerds. We're *all* different here.

But we only saw each other for a few hours a week. It wasn't like we were best friends.

Not the way Kacey and I had been.

Not even my friends at co-op were BFF-level close.

I wondered if there was still a way to make things right with Kacey.

PART THREE
Winter
ZZttz
BZZZzz
SKitter

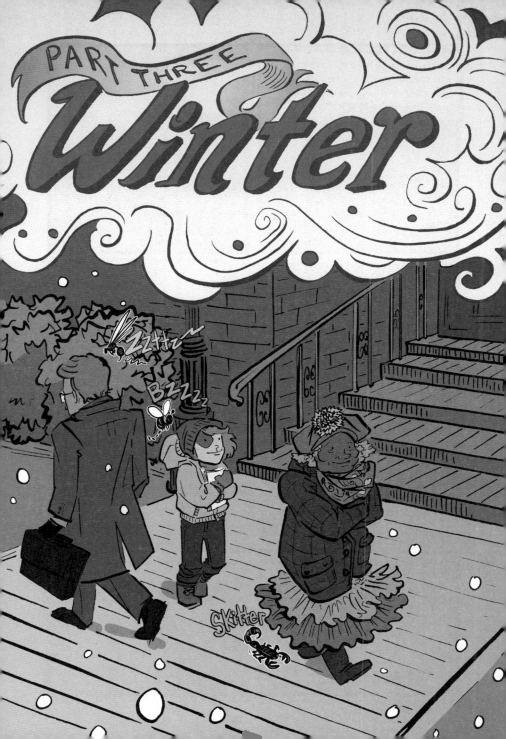

Whoo!

Snow!

138

So it's definite?

Yes.

Jerry will start up there in two weeks, but we won't follow till the new year.

What a whirlwind change for you and the girls!

It is, but I think it's for the best.

We'll be closer to my family in Connecticut.

That's Kacey's mom.

Poof!

Connecticut?

EXIT
Are . . .
you . . .
Moving to Connecticut?
BZZz
BZZz

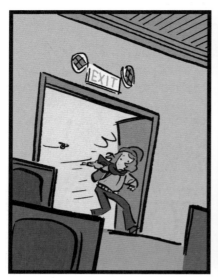

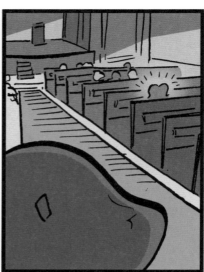

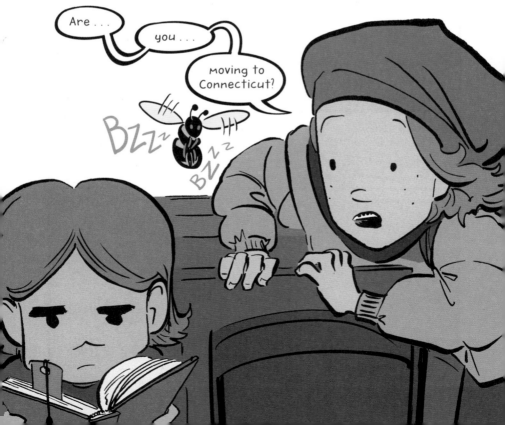

Yeah, my dad got a job there.

I had no idea.

Why would you? We don't talk anymore.

Now, if you don't mind, I've got a chapter to finish.

BZZZBZZZ
Everything okay?
It's tech week, that's all.
Well, I hope you don't get too worn out.
CHILDREN'S THEATRE
Remember, we've got your dentist appointment bright and early on Friday.
BZZBZZ BZZZ
BZZZ BZZZBZZZ BZZ BZZ
How could I forget?

Tech week—the final week of rehearsal before we performed—was lots of work.

We had to rehearse every single night, and on Thursday we moved to the opera house to work with sets and props and music cues.

Whoa.

By the end of each night, I was pooped.
WHOMP
ZZZZZ
Katie!
Did you sleep through your alarm?
We leave for the dentist in half an hour!
Poof
Poof
Poof
Poof
Poof
Poof

BZZZ BZZZ BZZZ
BZZZZ BZZ BZZ
One,
TAP
two,
TAP
three...
TAP
four
TAP
five
TAP
six
TAP
poof
...seven, eight, nine—
poof
TAP TAP TAP
Katie?
Dr. Kramer will be with you in a moment.

One,
two,
three.
BZZ BZZ
TAP TAP TAP
One, two, three.
BZZ BZZZZ
TAP TAP TAP
One,
two—
Hello there, Katie!
I hear we have some concerns about your lingual frenulum.
Such a fancy word, huh?
I suggested "tongue-string-a-ma-whoosit," but no one at the Global Dental Convention went for that.

Now let's take a look.

Open wide and lift that tongue?

Sure, Dr. Kramer was treating me like a kid, but he made me feel better.

Until . . .

Poof!

I'm inclined to agree with your orthodontist.

The frenulum isn't nearly as long as most, and it may inhibit your speech and swallowing abilities.

I recommend surgery.
I think it's the best path forward.
BZZZ BZZZ BZZ BZZ BZZ
I'm booked for the next few months, but Vera will get you scheduled for the next possible opening.
My worst fears had come true: Dr. Kramer was going to *chop off* part of my tongue.
Poof Poof Poof
No, no,
no—ow!
BZ BZZ Sting! BZZZ

The buzzing thoughts were getting worse.

One, two, three.

TAP TAP TAP

Are all your dresser drawers shut? You'd better check.

You have to check.

Ouch!

SLAM

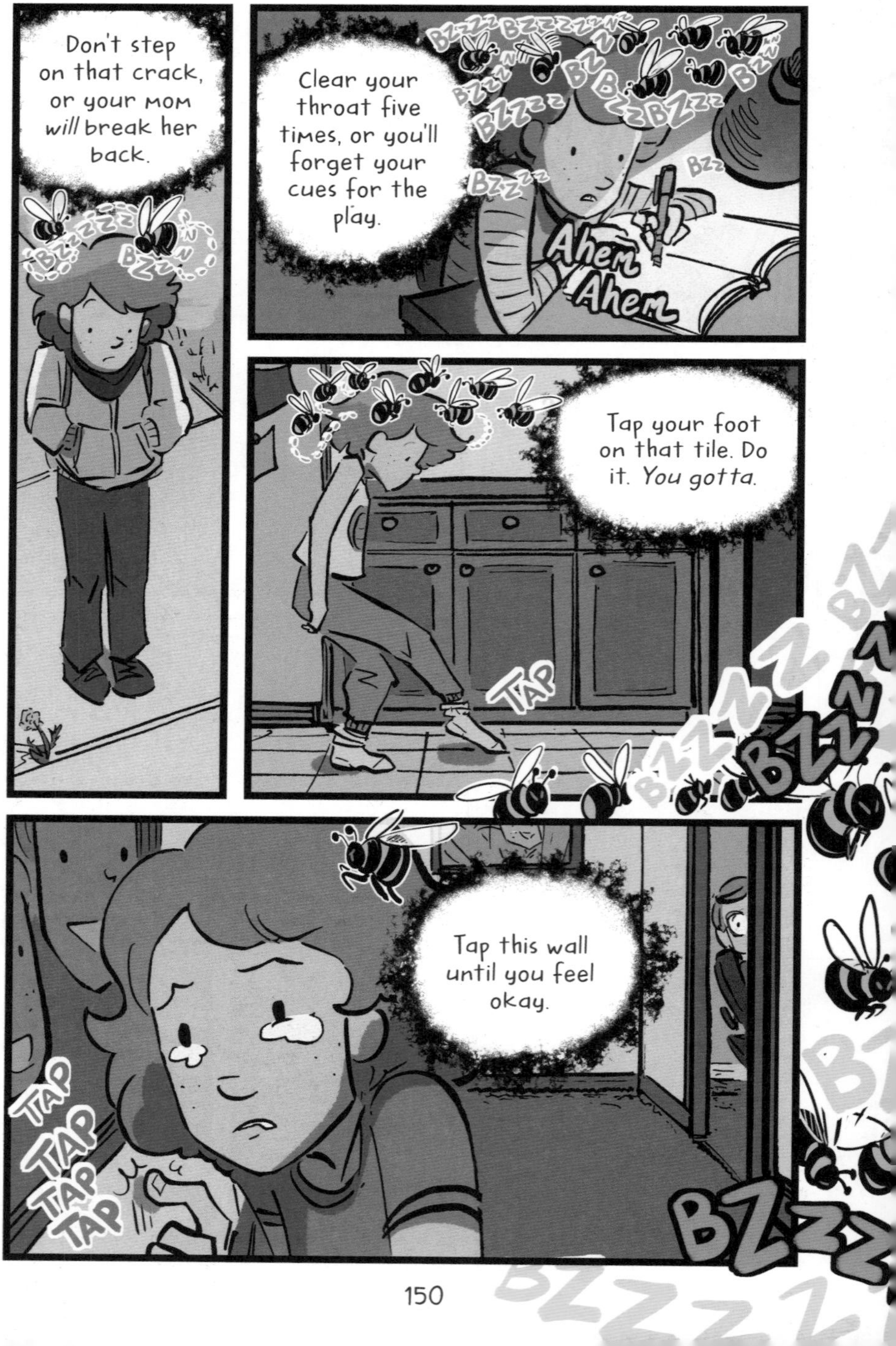

Don't step on that crack, or your mom *will* break her back.
Bzzzzz
Bzz
Clear your throat five times, or you'll forget your cues for the play.
Ahem
Ahem
Tap your foot on that tile. Do it. *You gotta.*
TAP
Tap this wall until you feel okay.
TAP
TAP
TAP
TAP
BZZZ

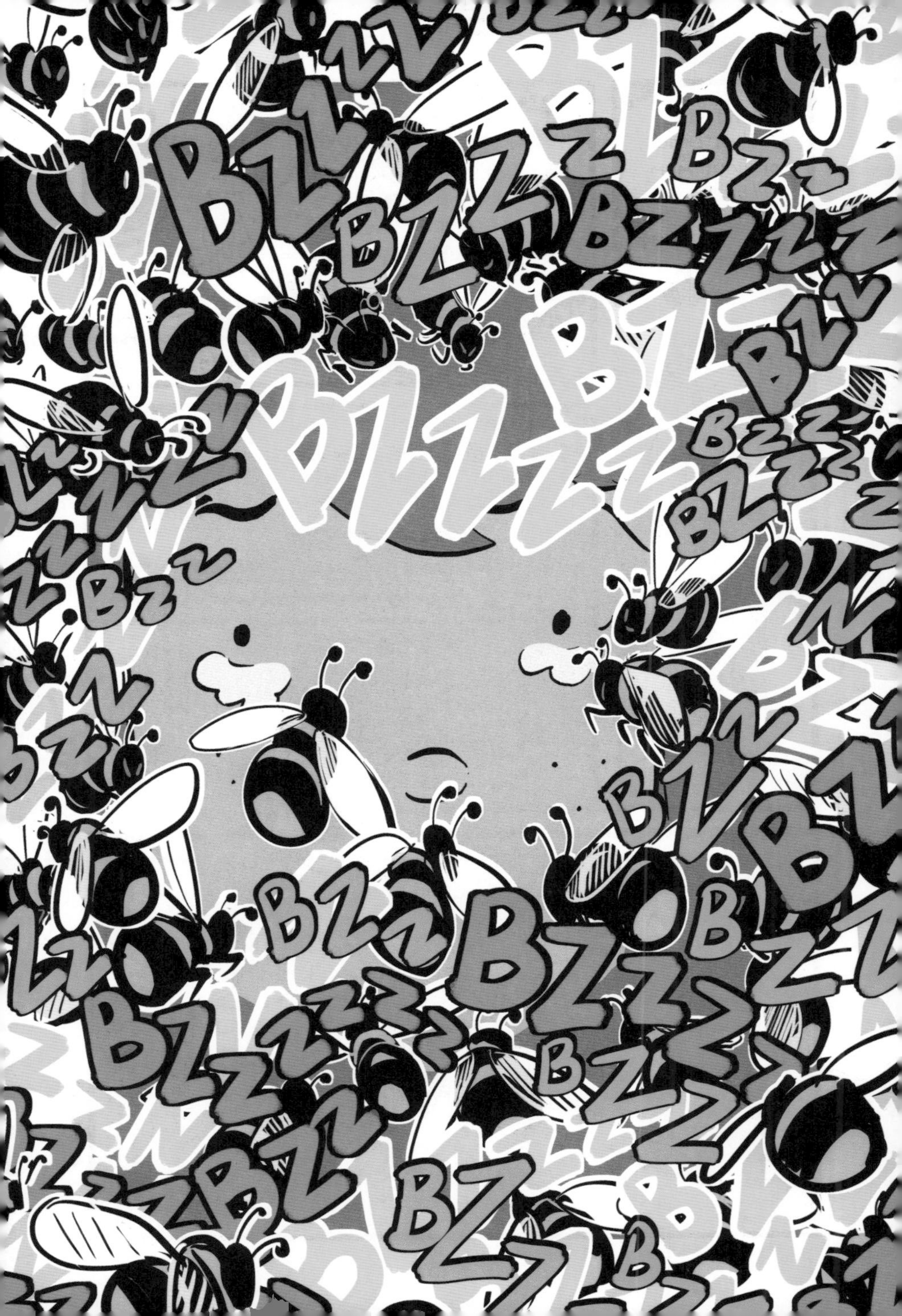

BZZ
BZZZZ
BZ
Bzz
BZZ
BZZ
BZZZZ
BZ

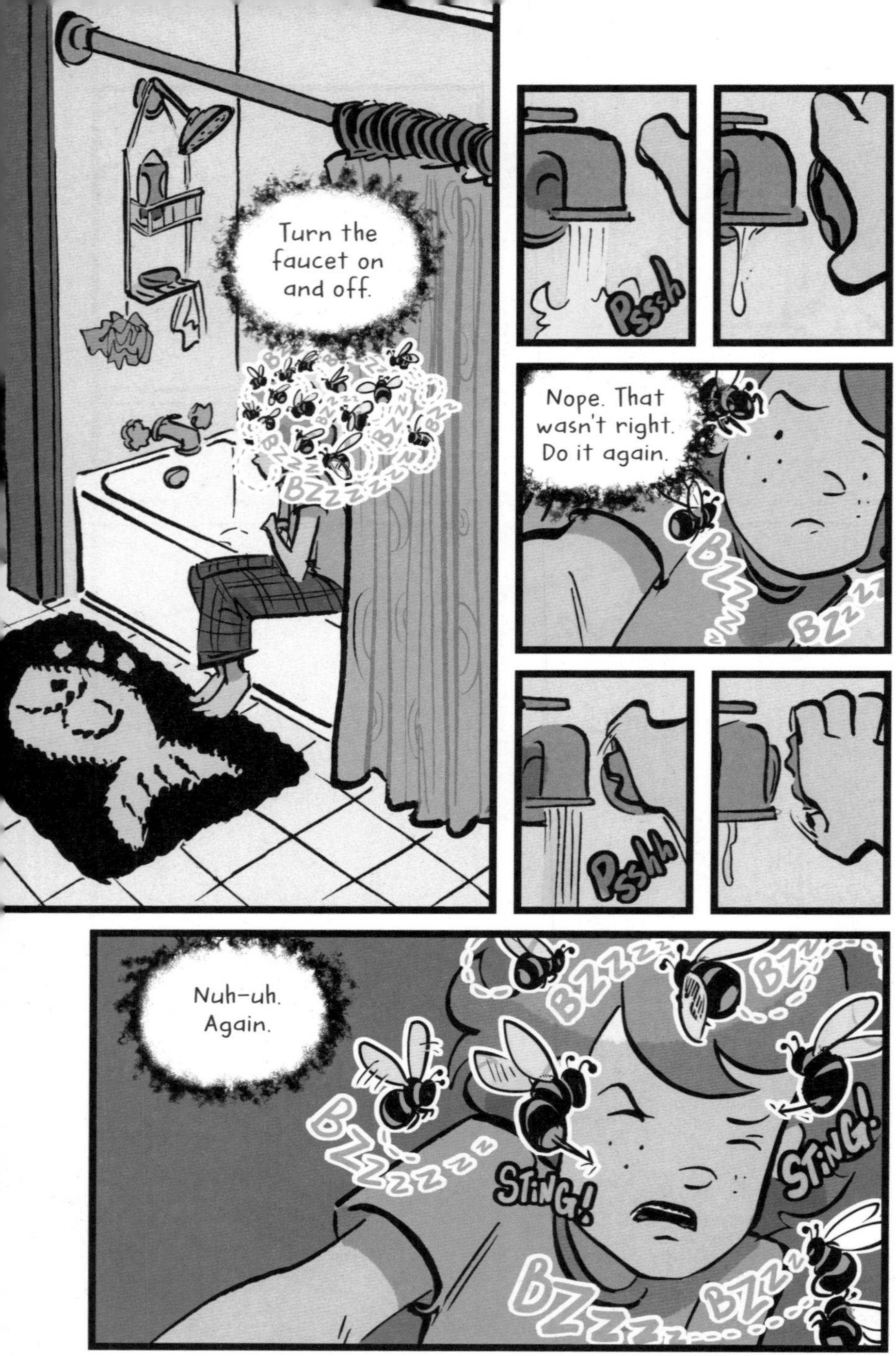
Turn the faucet on and off.
BZZZZZ
Psssh
Nope. That wasn't right. Do it again.
BZZ
BZZZ
Psshh
Nuh-uh. Again.
BZZZ
BZZ
BZZZZZZZ
STING!
STING!
BZZZZ
BZZ

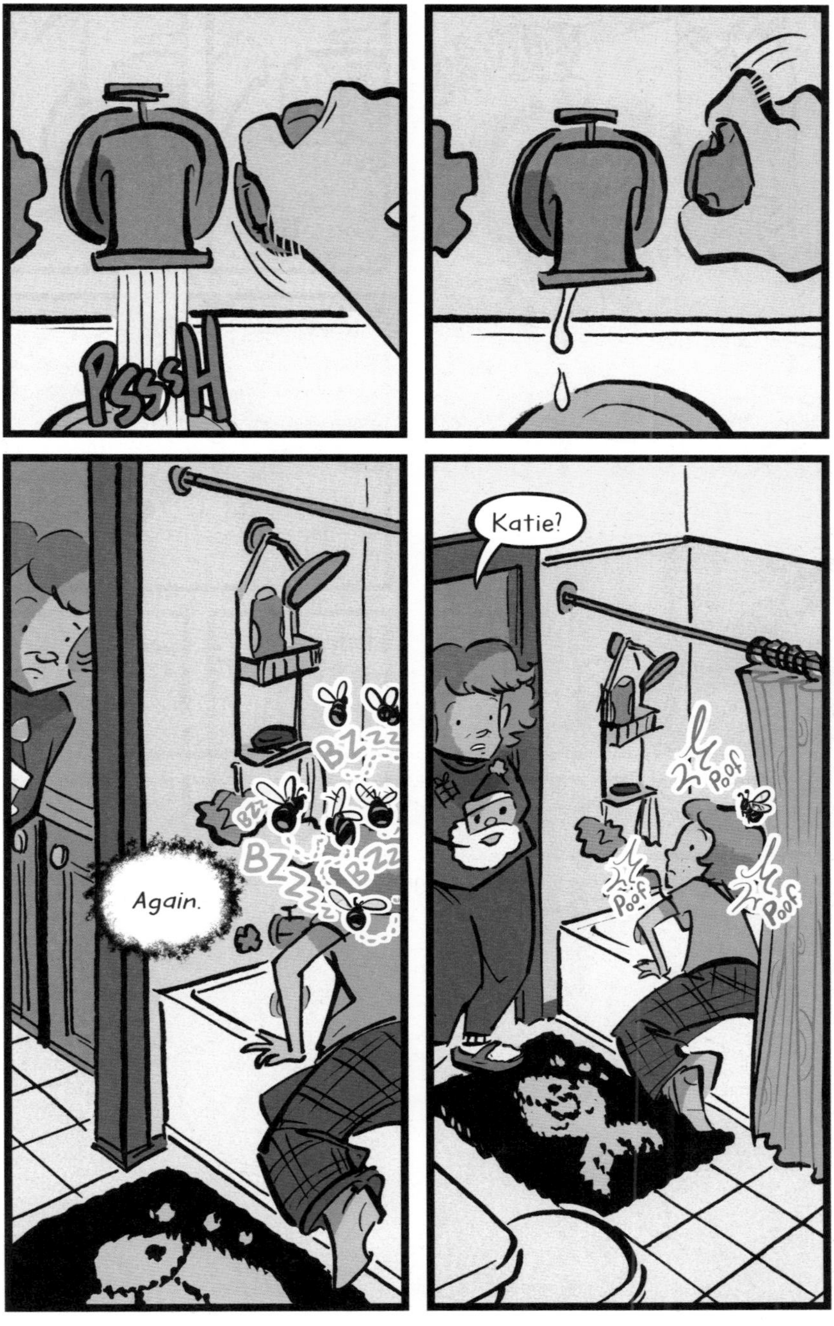
PSSSH
BZZ
BZZ
BZZ
BZZ
Again.
Katie?
Poof
Poof
Poof

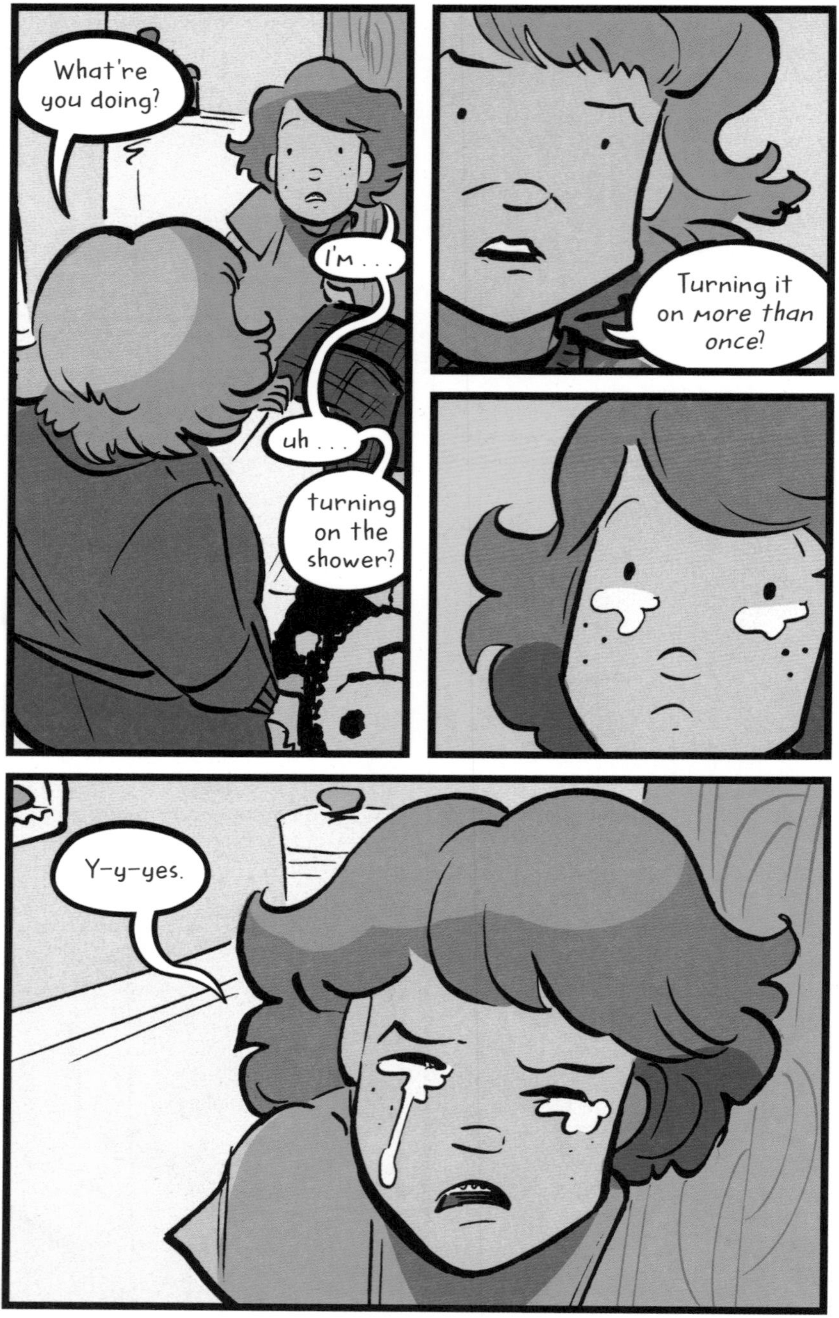
What're you doing?
I'm . . .
uh . . .
turning on the shower?
Turning it on more than once?
Y-y-yes.

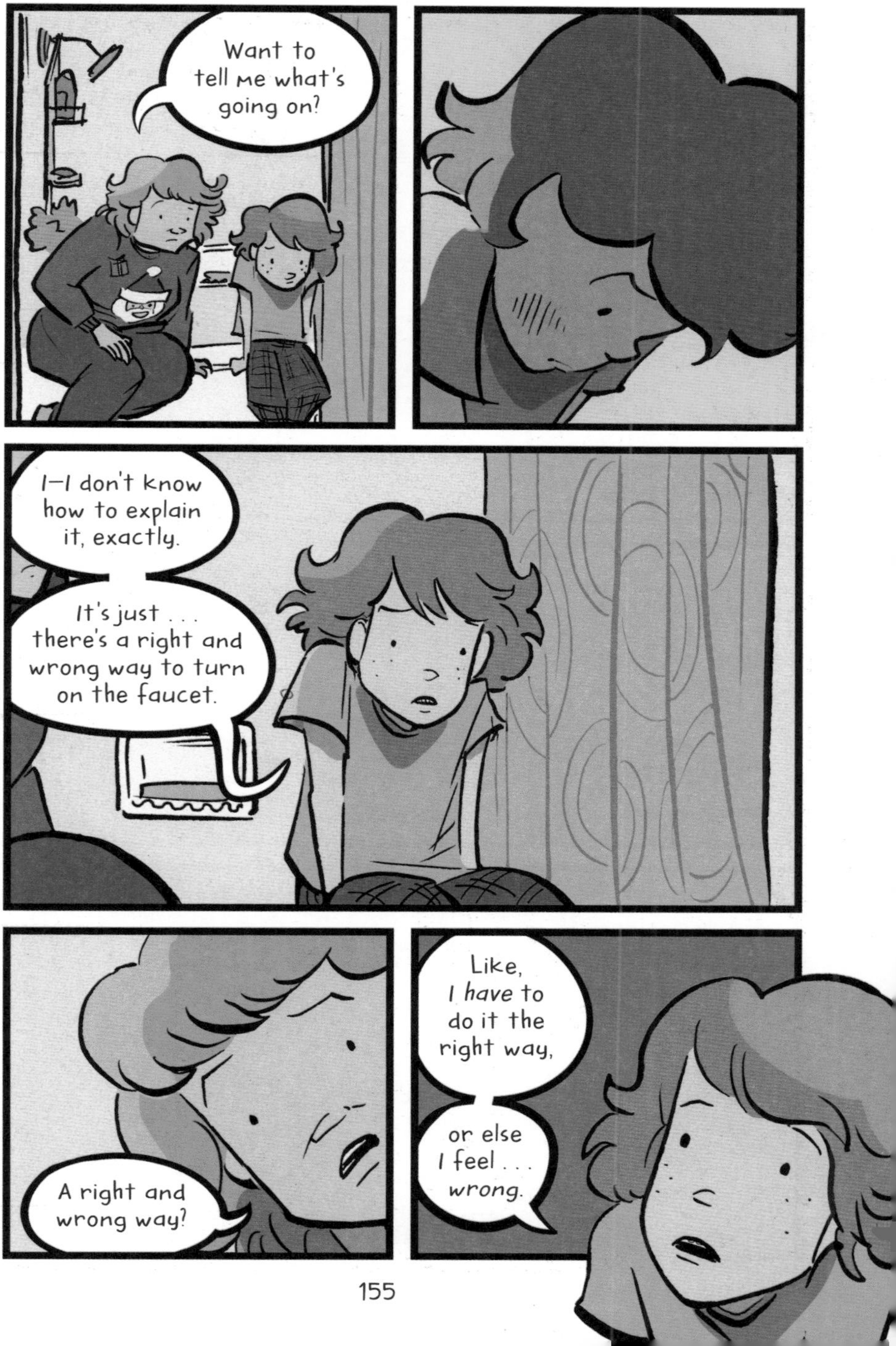
Want to tell me what's going on?
I-I don't know how to explain it, exactly.
It's just . . . there's a right and wrong way to turn on the faucet.
A right and wrong way?
Like, I *have* to do it the right way,
or else I feel . . . *wrong*.

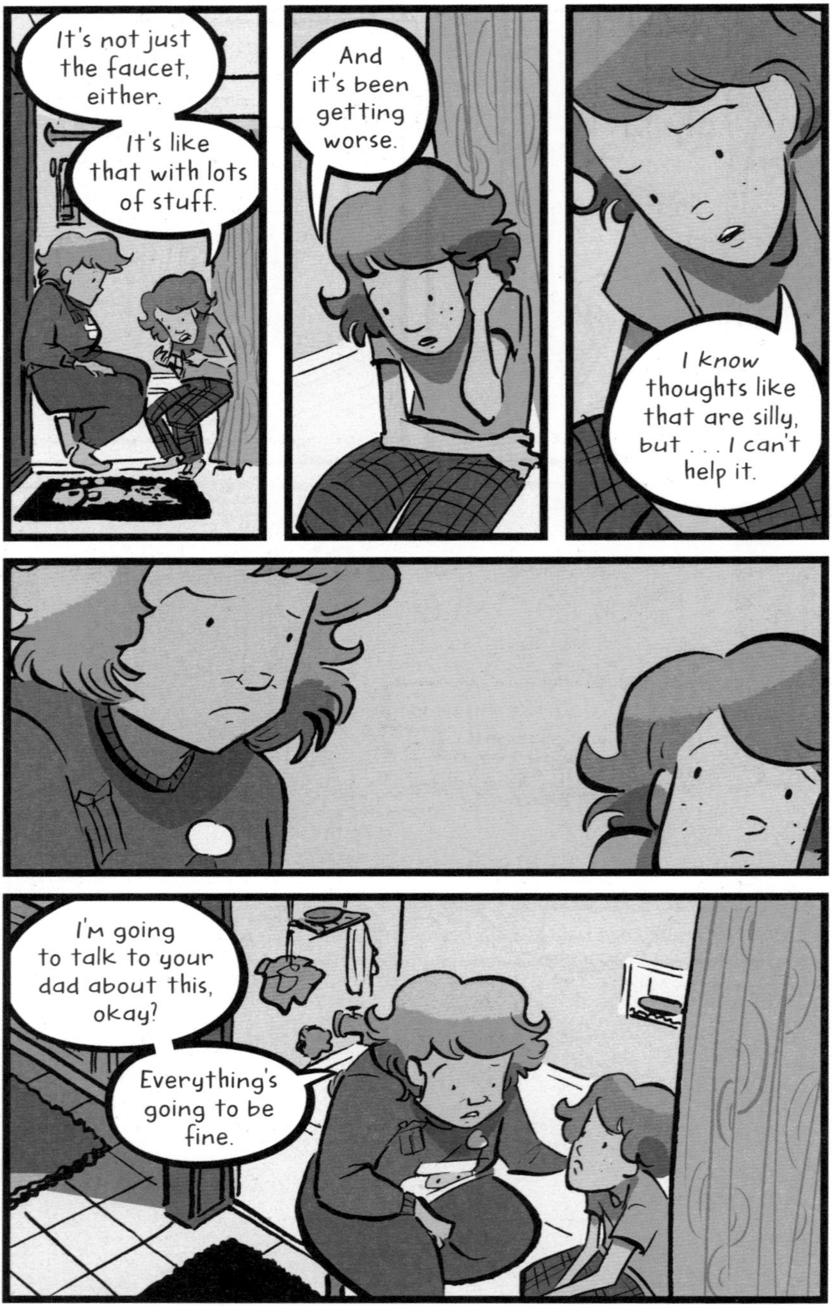
It's not just the faucet, either.
It's like that with lots of stuff.
And it's been getting worse.
I know thoughts like that are silly, but . . . I can't help it.
I'm going to talk to your dad about this, okay?
Everything's going to be fine.

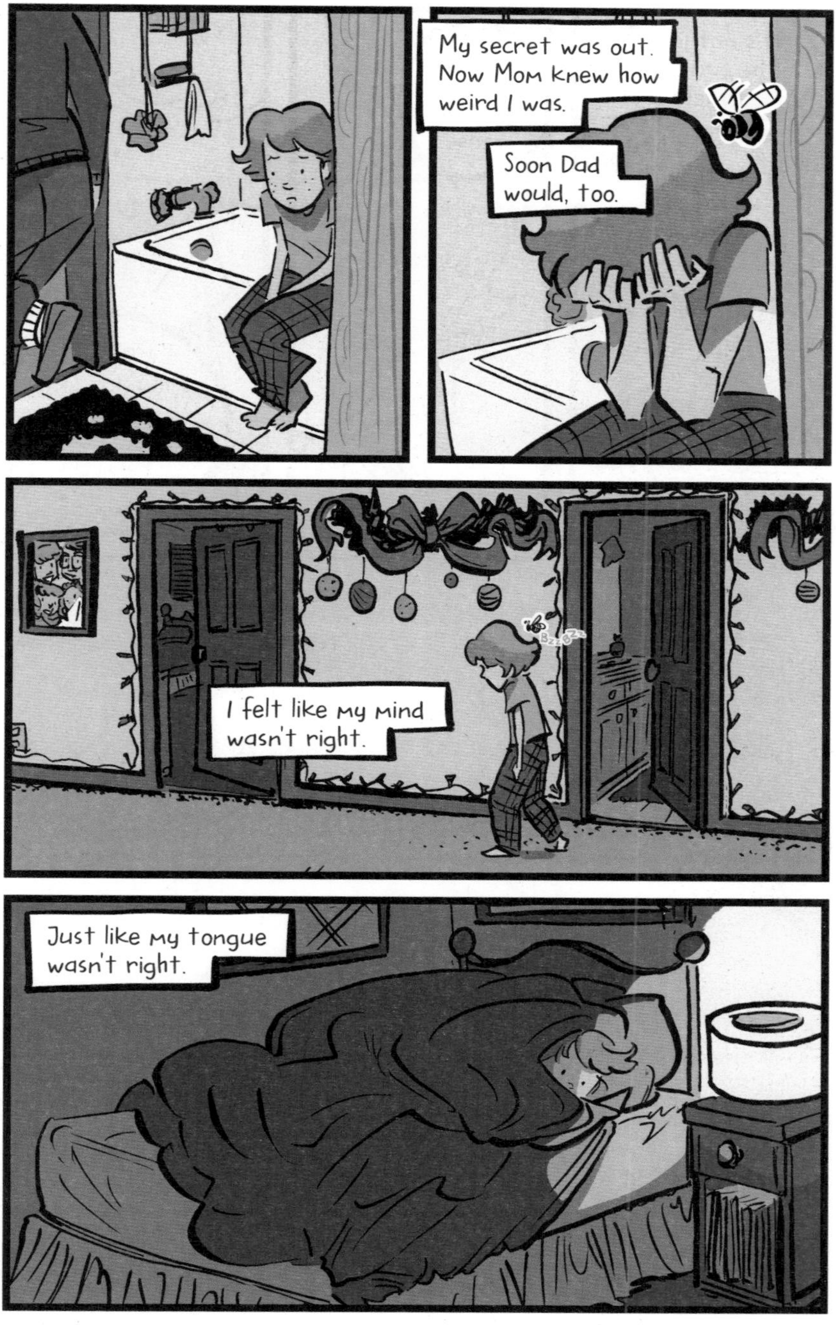
My secret was out. Now Mom knew how weird I was.
Soon Dad would, too.
Bzz
I felt like my mind wasn't right.
Just like my tongue wasn't right.

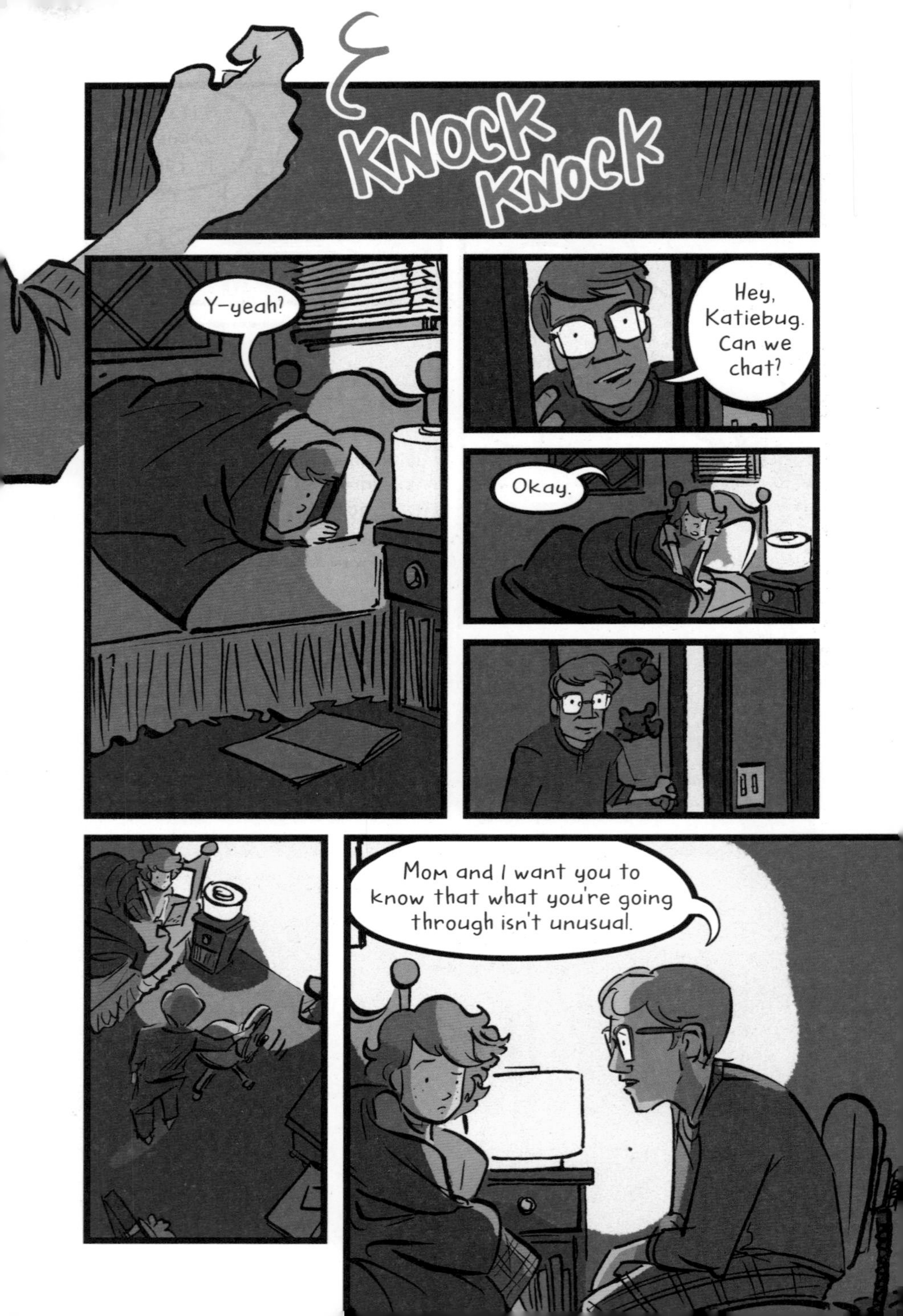
KNOCK KNOCK
Y-yeah?
Hey, Katiebug. Can we chat?
Okay.
Mom and I want you to know that what you're going through isn't unusual.

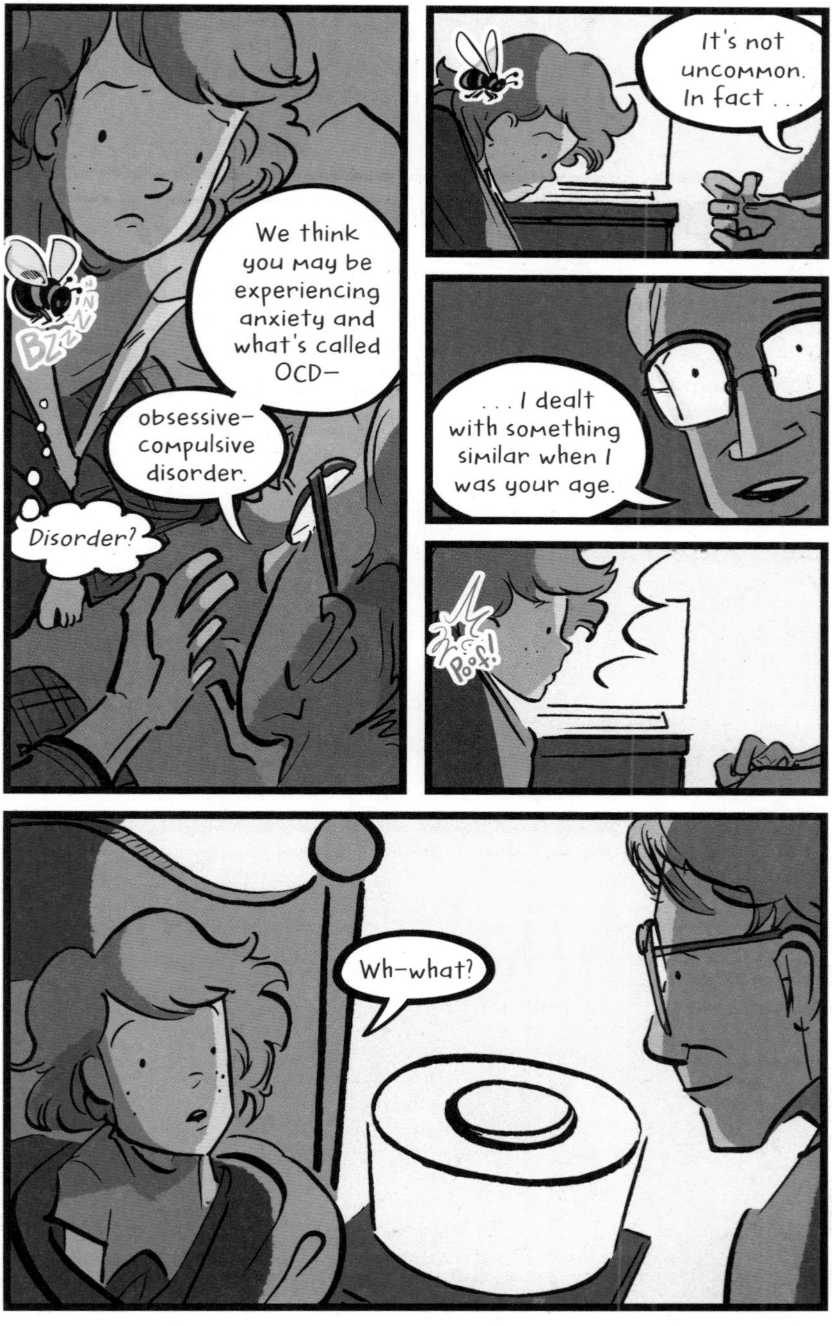
We think you may be experiencing anxiety and what's called OCD—
BZZZNNN
obsessive-compulsive disorder.
Disorder?
It's not uncommon. In fact . . .
. . . I dealt with something similar when I was your age.
Poof!
Wh-what?

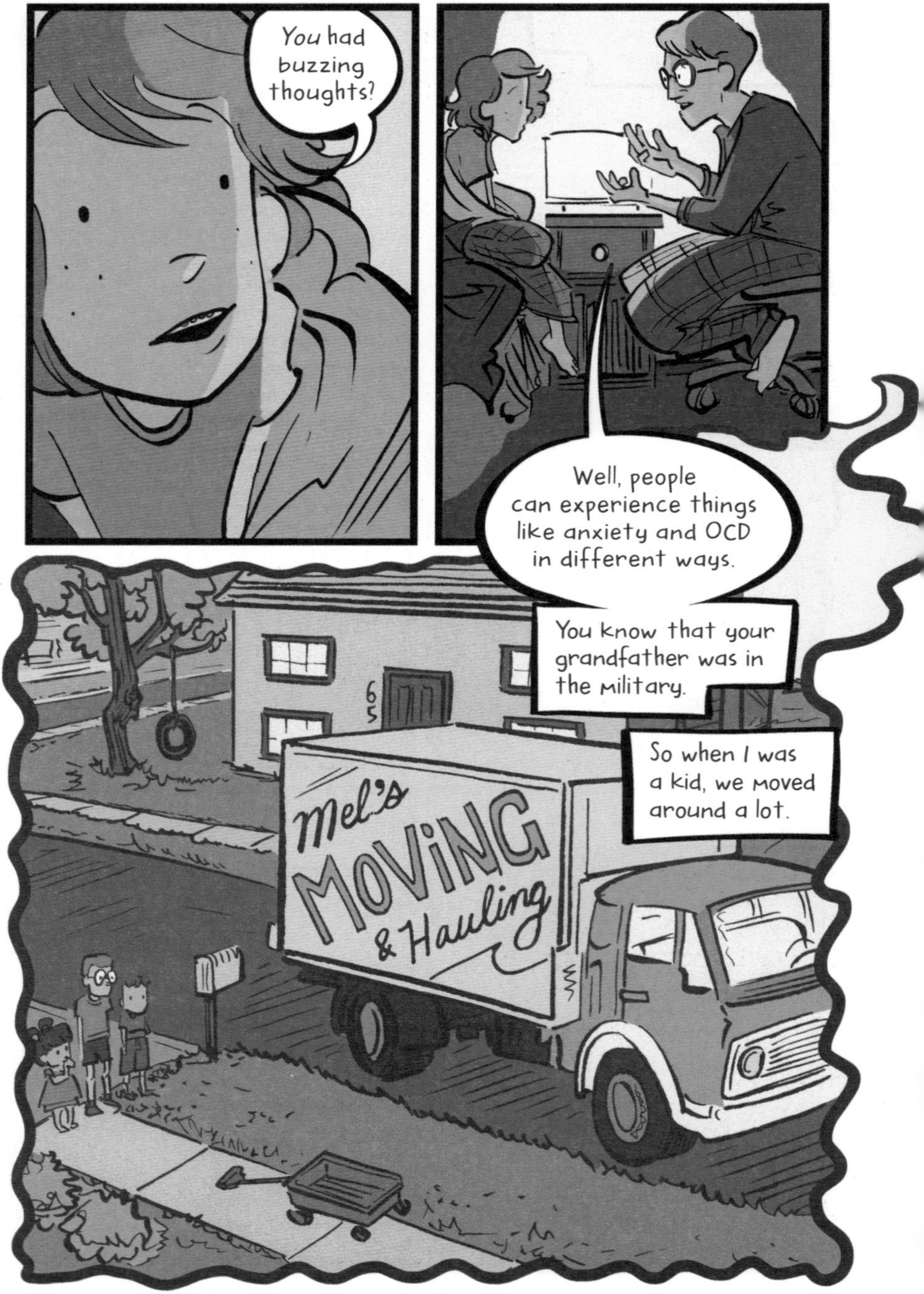

You had buzzing thoughts?
Well, people can experience things like anxiety and OCD in different ways.
You know that your grandfather was in the military.
So when I was a kid, we moved around a lot.
65
Mel's MOVING & Hauling

We moved to a new city almost every year.
I was constantly changing schools.
That made me really anxious.
HA
HA
HA
HA
HA
HA
HA
HA
HA
Poof!
My thoughts would even keep me up at night.
Chirp!
Chirp!
CHIRP
Chirp
CHIRP
CHIRP
CHIRP
CHIRP
CHIRP
CHIRP
CHIRP
CHIRP
CHIRP
CHIRP
CHIRP
CHIRP
CHIRP
CHIRP
CHIRP

My thoughts keep me up sometimes, too.

And I do a lot of weird stuff because of them.

It's not weird. Sometimes our minds are just wired in different ways.

How do you know for sure that I have OCD?

I don't.

But we can find a professional who will.

Poof!

A professional?

Bzzzz
Bzzz
Bzzzz
Bzzzz
Someone who knows a lot about these things, who can help you.
There's nothing wrong with you, Katiebug.
Plenty of people go through this.

It may take some time before we can get you an appointment.

Just like with Dr. Kramer, huh?

Yes. Like that.

BZZz
BZZz

For now, you can come to me and Mom with any problems.

Okay?

Okay.

This is so embarrassing.

I'll tell you something that *I* find helpful to remember:

Our thoughts aren't *us*. They're just thoughts.

They're neurons firing in our brains. They don't make us who we are.

So when thoughts upset you, or they make you want to do things you don't *really* want to do, remind yourself . . .

it's the thoughts talking, *not* Katie.

Thanks, Dad.

I didn't get it, though. My thoughts were my thoughts. How could some of them not be me?
And how could I ignore them?
I tried, but sometimes they just wouldn't leave me alone.

At least I had a name for the buzzing thoughts.

And that meant I wasn't the only one.

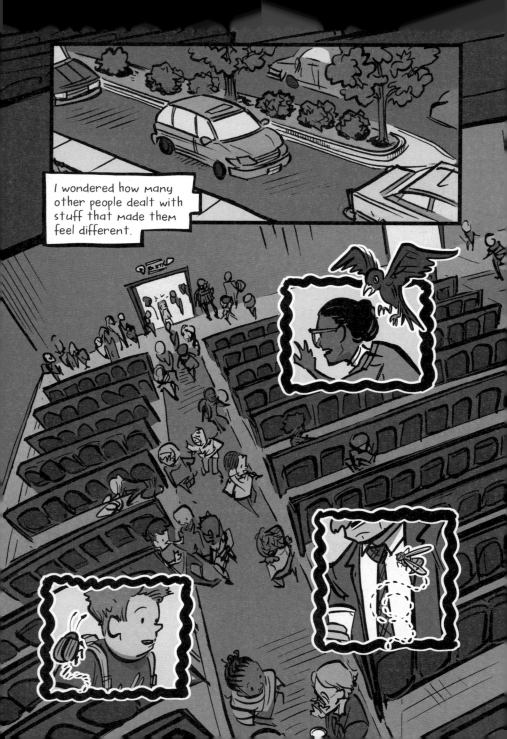

I wondered how many other people dealt with stuff that made them feel different.

What if we're *all* a little different?
JPL

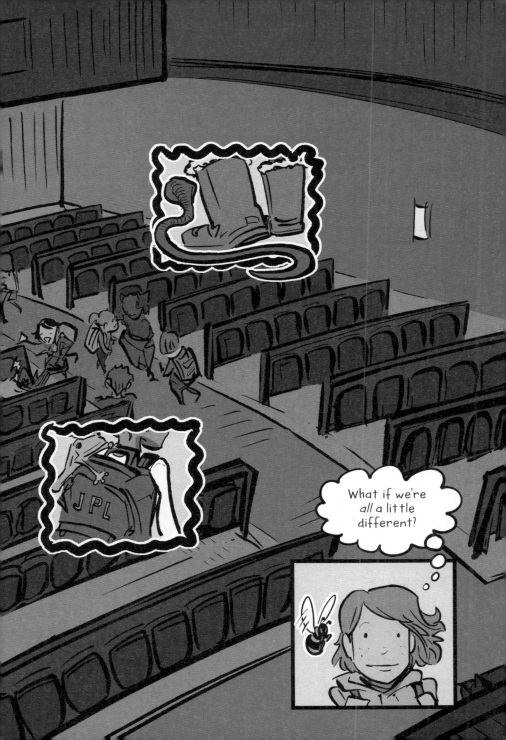

OPENING NIGHT
Opera House
OPENING NIGHT

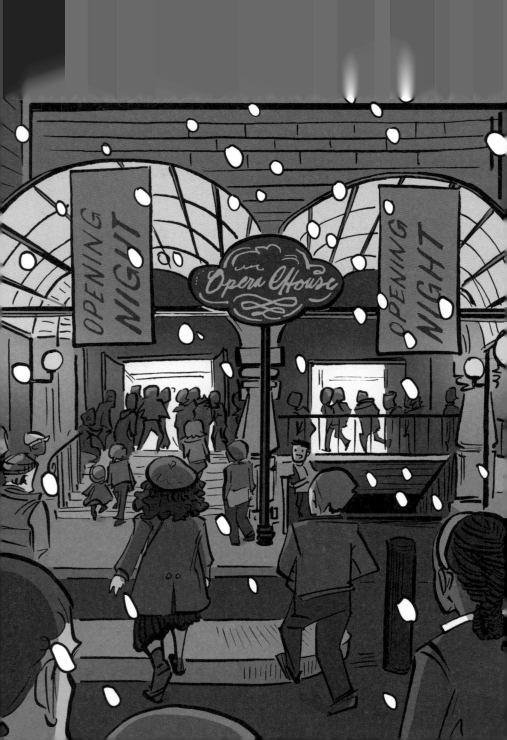

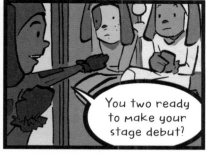

This is it, pups!

You two ready to make your stage debut?

BzzBzzz

Ready as we'll ever be.

Genevieve's puppies to the wings.

Here we go!

171

It was strange how, when it was filled with people, the opera house didn't seem so gigantic.
You couldn't make out the audience in the dark. It just felt like one big, elaborate rehearsal.
Except for the parts when people laughed or clapped.
Poo, poo.
HA HA HA HA HA HA HA HA HA HA HA HA HA HA HA
CLAP CLAP
WHOO!
CLAP

We did it!

Some of my co-op friends came to opening night.

It was sooo good!

You all were super-convincing puppies.

Thanks!

Kacey wasn't there, though.

She was probably getting ready for her big move in January.

After opening night, the show was in full swing.

We performed for schools on weekdays . . .

. . . and for the public on weekend days and nights.

The ADVENTURES of MADELINE
SUNDAY MATINEE
SOLD OUT

It was nothing but show business for two weeks straight.

Then, just like that, we'd given our final performance.

Wrap party 6PM
They should've called it a *holiday wrapping* party.
Missed opportunity.
'TIS THE Season to be Jolly
FA-LA-LA
I'm really going to miss you all.
Yeah. Team Genevieve forever.
But we've got each other's phone numbers!
We'll stay in touch.
And maybe we'll be in more plays together.

Paw for one . . .
And one for paw!
Let's get together in January!
For sure.
Yeah!
But I wasn't sure if any of us believed we would.
After all, Delaney and I hadn't stayed in touch after summer camp.

I still saw my co-op friends.

But the truth was, I wasn't close with any of them the way I had been with Kacey.

Our fight seemed so silly now.

That Friday, on our last co-op day before winter break . . .

Did you hear?

Kacey and her family moved early.

Kacey's gone.

I didn't get the chance to say goodbye.

Poof!

What if she hates me?

What if she goes on hating me forever?

BZzzz

BzzBzzz

BZz

BHC HOLIDAY PARTY

I should've apologized, and now it's too late . . .

BZzzz Bzzz

Bzzzz

C'mon, let's check out karaoke!
BZZZZZ
BZZZZZZZ
BZZ
BZZZ
Sure!
I'll be there in just a sec.
BZZ BZZ BZZZ
BZ BZZZ BZ
TAP
One, two, three.
TAP
TAP
TAP

TAP

I knew now that what I was doing was probably a "compulsion."

TAP

But knowing that didn't change much.

TAP one

Maybe the buzzing thoughts weren't me, but I still had to do what they said.

TAP two

That was what made me feel better.

More in control.

TAP three

Even if I wasn't, really.

PART FOUR
Spring
BZzzz
SUITE 220
DENTIS
J. KRAMEF

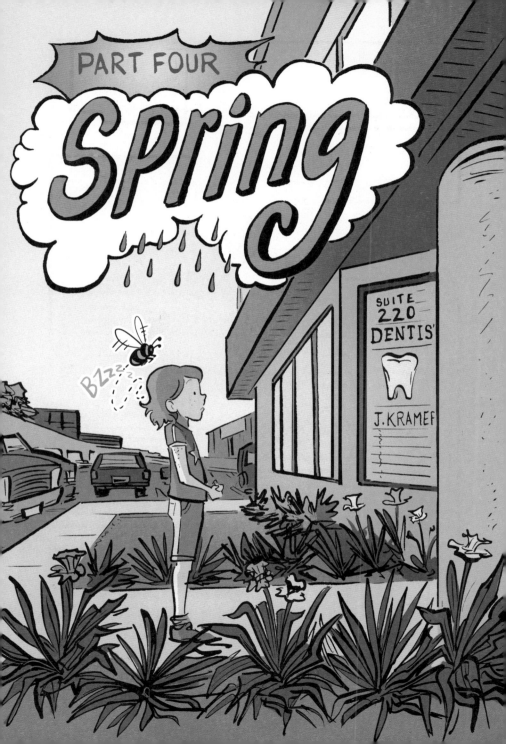

Three,
two,
one.

HAPPY NEW YEAR!
CLINK
CLink
SPARKLIN GRAPE JUICE
It was a new year.

But mostly . . .

. . . life stayed the same.

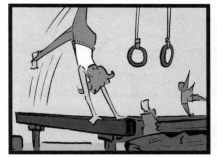

Estoy cansada.

Quiero azúcar.

Sí, por favor.

I did have two big appointments coming up, though.
JANUARY
Poof
Poof
flip
Katie's Lingual Frenectomy
24
Bzz
flip
flip flip
Katie's appt with Dr. Barnard
30
Bzz
B
Bzz

FAITH BAPTIST CHURCH
SUNDAY 10AM - 11AM

Shadrach
Meshach
and Abednego
SEVENTH GRADE SUNDAY SCHOOL

One morning in Sunday School, our teacher introduced a new student.

Everyone, this is Geneva Pasquel.

She and her family just moved here from Michigan.

You can call me Ginni.

I didn't have any good friends at church.

giggle

But Ginni seemed nice.

I'm Katie.

Hi.

CLASSROOMS

Those are my parents.

Oh! They're talking to my parents.

Those are my brothers, Adrien, Julien, and Valentin.

And this is my sister, Amalie.

She's a year younger than me.

Hi. Oh my gosh, I *love* your hair.

Is it naturally red?

O-oh, yes.

Well, of course! Silly me. You can tell, because your eyebrows are so light.

It's just divine. Like Rita Hayworth's.

Do you know Rita Hayworth?

Oh. No?

I'm *obsessed* with old Hollywood actresses.

My icon is Audrey Hepburn. One day, once Mama approves, I'm going to get my hair cut like hers.

Way up here.

I think that'd look good on you.

Well, Mama says I have the chin for it.

But for now, I'm going with more of an Elizabeth Taylor look.

I don't really like my haircut.

Oh, but it's pretty!

It looks like you girls are getting along well.

Absolutely.

Mr. and Mrs. Pasquel have been telling us that they also homeschool.

And they've moved in just down the street from us.

That's so cool.

We should set up a time for you girls to get to know each other better.

How about a visit to our place soon?

They seem really cool.

Sounds great.

Bye! See you soon!

Who was that?

Maybe my new best friends.

The next week, we paid a visit to the Pasquels.
Mom brought her famous Kentucky chocolate-walnut pie as a housewarming gift.
Hello! That smells *delicious.*
Katie, the girls are upstairs if you'd like to join them.
Poof!
BZzzZZ

You're here!

Ginni's been so boring all morning, reading her book.

I'm almost finished with this chapter.

ANNE OF GREEN GABLES

She's always saying that.

Anyway, I thought we could watch a movie together, if you want.

Have you ever seen *Calamity Jane*?

Um... no?

Oh, well, that's perfect! It'll be new to you.

I mean, if you *feel* like watching a musical.

How do you feel about musicals?

CLAP CLAP

Poof

I *love* them.

I also love *Anne of Green Gables.*

Really?

Yeah! The movie is great, too.

Oooh, we should watch it together next time!

Next time!

It was so fun hanging out with Ginni and Amalie.

I just blew in from the Windy City!

Ginni was quiet, but we talked about our favorite books.

Roll of Thunder, Hear My Cry

THE BLACK CAULDRON

THE GIVER

BRIDGE to TERABITHIA

Jacob Have I Loved

Amalie talked a *lot*. About old movies and musicals and fashion and makeup.

This shade is called Cerulean Sea. Doesn't that sound delicious?

Cerulean Sea.

What's your favorite musical?

Definitely Annie.

Thanks for having me over!

Mama will make crepes next time, okay?

And we'll have a tea party!

It's a time-honored tradition in the Pasquel home.

Sounds great!

I really like them.

Good!

Because I think Mrs. Pasquel is going to enroll them in the co-op next school year.

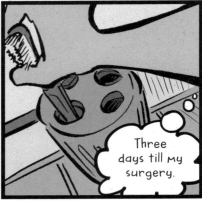

Three days till my surgery.

I can't believe that's going to be *gone* soon.

Poof

Poof

Mom said Dr. Kramer will give me a shot in the mouth.

BZZZZ

BZZ

BZZ

BZZ

BZZ

BZZZ

A SHOT.
IN THE MOUTH.
And I'll be awake for the whole thing.
BZZZ
poof
BZZZ
TAP TAP TAP TAP TAP TAP
one two three
And they'll have to sew stitches under my tongue.
TAP TAP TAP
one two three four five
I don't talk funny. I can still eat food. Why do I even need surgery?
BZZZ

It's not fair.
x/5 = 85
x = 425
BZZZ
BZZZZ
BZZZ
BZZZZ
BZZZ
It just isn't.
425
SMACK!
BZZZZ
BZZ BZ
NNN

Tongue, tongue, tongue.

Hi.

Hey.

Uh . . . you okay?

Why wouldn't I be?

I dunno.

You look sad about something.

You'll understand when you're older.

Yeah, guess so.

It's just . . . I had this friend who turned out to be *not* a great friend.

Really?

What'd she do?

I don't want to talk details.
Oh.
I lost a friend, too.
It was kind of the worst.
It *still* is.
Yeah.
I know what you mean.
So I guess that doesn't get better, even when you're older?
Doesn't seem to.

Munch
Munch
Munch
Munch
Hey, Ashley?
Yeah?
Do you think of me as a little kid?
Why would you think that?

Because you don't hang out with me anymore.

And you have your own bathroom now, so you don't have to be around me.

BZzz
BZz

Munch
Munch

I don't think you're a little kid.

You're just...

younger.

One day you'll get it.

I wish I knew what "it" was.

Hey. About your surgery?
CONCERT TOUR 1992
BZZZ BZZZ BZZZ
BZZZZ BZZZ BZZZZ
I know it's scary.
But it's going to be okay.
BZZZZ
Really?

Yeah.
And you'll get to eat tons of ice cream afterward.
BZZ
Poof
Thanks.
Sure thing.

It's the big day, Katiebug!

Y-y-yeah. The big day.

BZZZZ
220
DENTI
J. KRAM
BZZZZ
It's going to be all right.
Dr. Kramer said I can sit in the room for the procedure.
BZZZ
But what can Dad do if something goes wrong?
POOF
POOF
BNN
Or if Dr. Kramer snips too far?
BZZZ
BNN
BZZ
BZZ

BZzz
BZzz
Or if your mouth won't stop bleeding?
BZzzz
Poof!
BZzz
BZzzzz
Or they don't sew your stitches the right way?
BZzz
BZzz
BZzz
BZZZ
Or the shot doesn't numb you, and you feel everything?
BZzzzzz
Poof!

Good morning, Katie! Come on back.

Tap your thigh, quick! Five times!

One,

TAP

two,

TAP

three,

TAP

four,

TAP

five.

TAP

These thoughts aren't me. I don't have to do what they say.

 I sure felt like I did, though.

 One, two . . .

Still. It was nice to know I could *tell* myself the buzzing thoughts weren't the real Katie.

 three four five *Poof!*

 That was a first.

 All righty!

Do you remember Donna from last time?

She'll be helping us out today.

Good morning, Katie.

Before we begin, I want to be sure you understand the procedure.

First, we'll be numbing your mouth with a shot.

Then we'll be removing that string beneath your tongue—

the lingual frenulum.

Once that string is gone, we'll sew a few stitches.

And these are very cool stitches.

They'll dissolve over time, right in your mouth.

Does all that make sense?

Y-yes. My parents told me what to expect.

Great! Any questions for me?

Will it hurt a lot?

What if something goes wrong??

Will you accidentally cut off my tongue???

I'm good.

All righty, then! First comes the shot.

It's okay if you want to close your eyes.

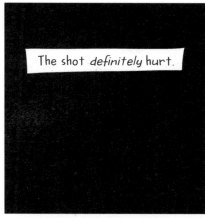

The shot *definitely* hurt.

But not as much as I thought it would.

It was weird, watching Dr. Kramer and Donna work on my mouth.

But also kind of . . . cool?

Everything was going well until . . .

SNiP!

Is Dad okay?

All done. Say goodbye, lingual frenulum!

This girl deserves plenty of ice cream.

It turned out that Dad *had* puked.
I normally have a strong stomach. I guess it's different when it comes to my daughter.
giggle
It was weird getting used to my mouth.
I had to stop myself from running my tongue along the stitches all the time.
nudge
But it was over. I'd done it!
No more buzzing thoughts about my lingual frenectomy *ever*.

I had to be careful about what I ate for a while, and I stayed home for a couple of days, recovering.

Hey there!

I finally got that film developed from summer camp.

Oh. Th-thanks.

Camp Aldridge.

It felt like all that stuff had happened ages ago.

MESS HALL

I wonder what you're up to in Connecticut.
I wish I'd said sorry.
At first, I wanted to stash the photos away.
Throw them away, even.

But then I decided I didn't want to forget that summer.

Kacey was still important to me.

She always would be.

As my tongue healed, the dogwoods bloomed.

School was almost over.

CHirp! CHirp!

And as every Kentuckian knew, the first Saturday of May meant . . .

KENTUCKY DERBY!

OUR COMPREHENSIVE LIST OF CONTESTANTS INSIDE

Ginni and Amalie had invited me to their house for a Derby sleepover.

I'd made my very own Derby hat for the occasion.

This was my first official Kentucky Derby party.
Normally, my family and I watched the race on TV at home, rooting for whichever horse we'd picked to win.
But today I'd be watching the Derby in style.
SWISH
Welcome to our private soiree, *dahhhling*!
Forgive my sister's lack of hat.
She prefers to keep things casual.
I prefer to keep things *comfortable*.

Oh, but your hat is *divine*.

You must dish about where you found this talented milliner.

Amalie made almost everything feel dramatic.

I liked that.

I also liked how straightforward Ginni could be.

They were the perfect pair of friends.

Now, since we're new to the state, you must tell us how this whole *Derby* sensation works.

This is our guide.

KENTUCKY DERBY CONTESTANTS

We each choose a different horse to root for.
This list shows who their owners and trainers are, the jockeys' names, *and* their odds of winning.
KENTUCKY DERBY CONTESTANTS
This year, Point Given is the favorite.
That's the horse most people think is going to win.
POINT GIVEN
#1
But I like rooting for the underdogs.
Like, say, Talk Is Money.
His odds aren't great.
KENTUCKY
They've got such funny names. Look at this one: Songandaprayer!
KENTUCKY DERBY
And Dollar Bill? What kind of names are these?
Derby names.

HMMM.

KENTUCKY CONTESTANTS

I choose Monarchos.

It's actually a pretty name.

I pick Thunder Blitz!

I place my *imaginary* bet on Invisible Ink!

Now it's a matter of waiting.

And *eating*. Mama's going to make her crepes!

What do you normally eat at a Derby party?

Definitely pie. Sometimes burgoo, biscuits, and beer cheese.

And also mint juleps, but we're too young for those.

They've got alcohol in them.

Oooh.

Well, we *can* do this.

Ta-da! Mint water-ups!

What are you girls up to?

Making age-appropriate beverages.

Very clever.

Now clear out of here. I've got crepes to whip up.

They're our great-grandmother's recipe, and they're *delicious.*

CLICK

The Derby always starts at six o'clock on the nose.

You've got to tune in on time, because it's over in two minutes.

That fast?

Yep.

AND THEY'RE OFF!

Go, Invisible Ink!

Come on, Thunder Blitz!

MONARCHOS!

Jorge Chavez and Monarchos have won the Kentucky Derby!

He was as fast as Secretariat!

MONARCHOS! MONARCHOS!

These are so good, Mrs. Pasquel.

I've never had a crepe before.

Never?

Well, I'm glad my grandmother's recipe was your very first taste.

Me too.

Mom says we got accepted into BHC for next year.

It's going to be so great to have you there.

And we're gonna do so much cool stuff together this summer!

I have a video recorder.
We could make our own movie next time we hang out.
It could be based on *Anne of Green Gables*!
Oooh, yes!
And I can be in charge of costumes and makeup.
We could call it . . . *Anne of Kentucky*!
YES!
Let's start writing a script.
ANNE OF KENTUCKY

Thanks again for having me over.

Anytime!

Want to hang out again next weekend?

Oh. Um . . .

BZzzz

Poof

BZZzz

I can't.

My friend Jaime invited me to go to Kentucky Kingdom that day.

BZZz

BZZzz

Will they get mad at me for hanging out with another friend?

Oh, fun! I love theme parks.

Poof

Is Jaime one of your friends from the co-op?

230

Um, yeah.

She's great. I can introduce you to her when co-op starts.

That'd be *divine*.

They didn't get mad.

Maybe I could have best friends *and* good friends.

I didn't have to choose.

And I didn't feel like a kid for not knowing all the "cool" movies and music around Amalie and Ginni.

I could just be me.

Poof

But would your friends like you if they knew about the buzzing thoughts?

HA HA HA HA HA HA HA HA HA HA HA HA HA HA HA HA

I don't know.

But I think they might.

MEDICAL PLAZA
The next day I had an appointment.
No braces or lingual frenectomies this time. I was going to a new kind of doctor.
One who could help me with the buzzing thoughts.
Poof
BZz
BZZ
Poof
B
Poof
ZZZZ

Bzzzz
You can't step on those cracks or Amalie and Ginni will stop being friends with you.
Bzzzzzzz
BZZZZZZZZ
Or you'll get in a car wreck on the way home.
BZZZZZZZZ
Or Dr. Kramer will discover
something else wrong
with your mouth.
These are just thoughts.
They're not me.

You all right, Katiebug?

Not really.

It's okay if you're nervous.

I would be, too.

But Dr. Barnard's job is to help you, just like Dr. Kramer helped with your tongue.

Only, no shots this time.

So she'll make my buzzing thoughts go away?

Well, they might not *go* away.

But I think Dr. Barnard can help you learn ways to live with those thoughts.

How to talk back to them.

She'll be able to help you in ways that Mom and I can't.

Whatever happens, you're going to be okay.

BZZZ
BZZZZ
BZZZZ
I still didn't step on the cracks . . .
. . . but I felt a little better than I had before.
I didn't feel like I was so different.
MEDICAL PL
BZZZ
SQUAWK
SQUAWK
chirp
chirp

Or alone.
Skitter
Skitter

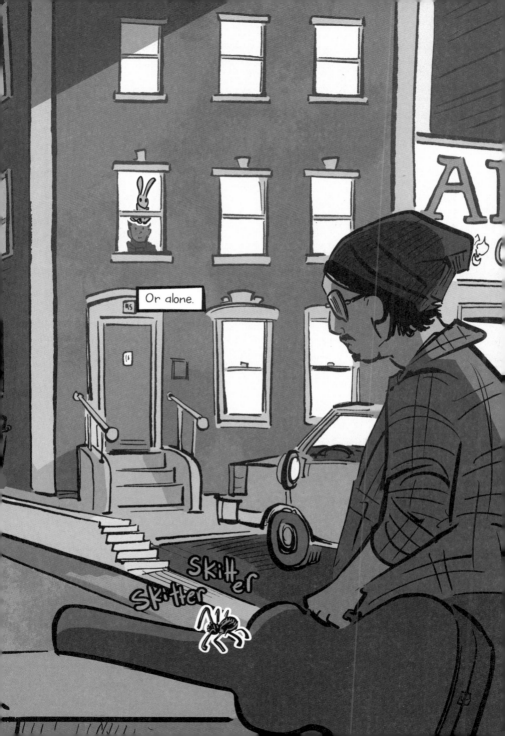

STE 102
DR. CLARA BARNARD
PSYCHOLOGIST
And even though I wasn't sure what lay in store for me . . .

. . . I was ready to find out.

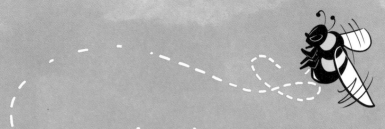

Author's Note

Growing up, I loved to read. Just like Katie, I devoured stories like *Annie*, *Madeline*, and *Anne of Green Gables*, which all featured kick-butt redheaded heroines. Those stories made me feel a little less weird about my bright red hair, but I didn't know of any books that showed what it was like to be homeschooled, or what a lingual frenectomy was, or how to better understand my anxious and obsessive thoughts.

The contents of this book—from Katie's trip to summer camp to her bad haircut to her struggle with OCD—are based on my own experiences growing up. However, there are some differences between Katie's story and mine. I condensed real events that happened over a few years into just one year for Katie and filled in the gaps of my memory with invented details and conversations that best captured my remembered experience. I also changed the real-life names of everyone in the novel but mine, to protect their privacy and because this is just my story, from my perspective. The characters in Katie's story were inspired by wonderfully multidimensional people, and I can't possibly do justice to any of them through this single lens of a story.

Younger me with braces on my four front teeth.

While Katie sees a mental health professional at the end of the novel, I didn't see a therapist until I was a senior in high school. I was nervous about going to that first appointment, even at seventeen. No one I knew talked much about mental health, and I felt the same way about therapy as I'd once felt about my OCD: that I was alone, and no one else got what I was going through. But . . . that wasn't true! My therapist was kind and knowledgeable. I found out that I wasn't the only one my age with OCD, that my thoughts didn't make me a "freak," and that there's absolutely nothing strange about seeing a therapist. In fact, doing so made my life a whole lot better.

People can experience obsessive-compulsive disorder in lots of different ways and with varying degrees of intensity. How my OCD manifested and how I responded to it might be very different from someone else's experience. Here are a few things OCD isn't, though: *Just being really clean and organized. Just* being a "germaphobe." Just being very particular. Sometimes people refer to these behaviors or traits as "OCD" without knowing what OCD means. It can be confusing to hear folks talk like that! Fortunately, there are many *unconfusing* resources out there to help you better understand your mental health, including the International OCD Foundation (iocdf.org) and the Anxiety and Depression Association of America (adaa.org).

I'll be honest: Writing *Growing Pangs* was a little scary for me. I was writing about my own life, after all! But I wanted to tell a story I wish I'd had when I was Katie's age, which showed how completely normal it is to go through changing friendships, to get unexpected dental procedures, and to experience what

Younger me rockin' on the piano. My hair had grown out
a little here since that awful haircut.

I call my "buzzing thoughts." And it's okay to reach out to
someone when you need help. You can tell a parent or trusted
adult about what you're going through, and together you can
decide what's best to do, which might include—like it did for
me!—seeing a licensed mental health professional.

If you're experiencing something that makes you feel
different from everyone else, please know that you're not
alone. There are others who have gone through or are going
through similar things, and there are people who can
understand and help, from friends to family members to
teachers to other trusted adults. You deserve the chance
to tell your own important, valuable story, and you deserve
to be heard!

ARTIST'S NOTE! BY MOLLY BROOKS

Hi THERE!
I'M MOLLY.
I DREW THE PICTURES IN THIS BOOK.

Scully, cat #1

AND EVEN THOUGH KATIE'S STORY ISN'T MY STORY...

IT'S ACTUALLY PRETTY SIMILAR TO MINE.

12-YEAR-OLD MOLLY

• Bad haircut
• Braces
• Loves books
• OCD

Cardigan, cat #2

THE THINGS KATIE DOES BECAUSE THE BUZZING THOUGHTS ARE TELLING HER SHE _HAS_ TO DO THEM ARE CALLED **COMPULSIONS**

O BSESSIVE (over and over)

C OMPULSIVE (have to do it)

D ISORDER (causes you problems)

I HAD THOSE, TOO. BUT I DIDN'T PICTURE THEM AS BEES—

I IMAGINED THERE WERE STRINGS ATTACHED TO ME THAT NO ONE ELSE COULD SEE.

BUT THEY **PULLED** AT ME.

If _I_ WANTED TO GO IN ONE DIRECTION, BUT THE STRINGS WERE PULLING ME IN A DIFFERENT DIRECTION..

Dad   Mom   Eric

I HAD TO DO A COMPLICATED SERIES OF MOVEMENTS TO REARRANGE THE STRINGS, SO I WOULD HAVE ENOUGH SLACK TO GO WHERE I WANTED TO.

① ② ③ ④

Coming!

If I DIDN'T DO IT RIGHT, THE STRINGS WOULD GET TIGHTER AND TIGHTER, THE MORE I TRIED TO GO AGAINST THEM.

Hrk!

MAYBE THEY WOULD TANGLE.

MAYBE THEY WOULD **SNAP.**

THUNK!

OR MAYBE THEY WOULD PULL ME APART.

It WAS REALLY SCARY.

SO I ALWAYS FOLLOWED THE STRINGS, AND I TRIED TO KEEP IT A SECRET.

BECAUSE I WAS EMBARRASSED ABOUT HOW WEIRD IT WAS, AND OF HOW SCARED I WAS.

BUT EVENTUALLY I FOUND A THERAPIST, AND SHE HELPED.

LATER I STARTED TAKING MEDICINE, AND THAT HELPED, TOO.

I LEARNED HOW TO MAKE THE STRINGS LONGER,

THEN WEAKER,

THEN EVEN TO IGNORE THEM COMPLETELY.

SO IF YOU HAVE STRINGS— OR BUZZING THOUGHTS, OR ANYTHING LIKE THAT— YOU DON'T HAVE TO BE SCARED, AND YOU DON'T HAVE TO KEEP IT A SECRET.

THERE ARE WAYS TO MAKE IT BETTER, AND PEOPLE WHO WANT TO HELP YOU.

Phoebe, cat #3

END.

247

Acknowledgments

All my thanks to Beth Phelan, who first suggested the idea of writing a graphic novel—something I hadn't thought possible before. You championed Katie's story from beginning to end, and I'm both grateful and gobsmacked to be on our *eighth* book together. Thank you, too, to the marvelous folks at Gallt & Zacker for your ongoing help and support.

My endless thanks to Shana Corey and Polo Orozco, an editorial dream team. I knew from the moment you shared your own magnificent childhood photos with me that you were going to take the best care of Katie's story. Thank you for your incisive edits and important questions, your compassion and care, your wit and humor, and your unbridled enthusiasm for this novel. You saw *Growing Pangs* through 2020, and that feat alone is parade-worthy. Thank you for always making me feel heard, understood, and encouraged as you turned my story into this graphic novel.

Thank you to Molly Brooks for illustrations that left me awestruck for 240 pages straight. Your talent bowls me over, Molly, and I consider myself the luckiest author on earth that you agreed to bring Katie's story (and the early 2000s of our childhoods) to life on the page. Thank you to Bex Glendining and Elise Schuenke for the stunning color you injected into this book. I grinned a mile long when I saw the first panel you'd finished, and I haven't stopped smiling about your work since.

Thank you to Dr. Julianna Sapienza for lending your expertise and tremendously helpful professional feedback to this manuscript. My thanks to both the International OCD Foundation and the Anxiety and Depression Association of America for providing resources that I have used both personally and professionally. And thank you to my therapists, both past and present, for the invaluable work that you do.

Thank you, *thank you* to the immensely talented Terri Libenson, Jennifer L. Holm, Matthew Holm, and Faith Erin Hicks for providing blurbs so kind that they knocked me right off my feet.

Many thanks to the brilliant folks at Random House Children's Books who worked to turn a color-coded Word document into an honest-to-goodness book. Thank you to April Ward for the gorgeous design work and to both Melinda Ackell and Alison Kolani for being copyediting heroes.

A warm thank-you to Janet Foley and Jen Jie Li, as well as to the fantastic individuals in marketing, publicity, and sales: John Adamo, Adrienne Waintraub, Kristin Schulz, Erica Stone, Shaughnessy Miller, Kelly McGauley, Janine Perez, Nicole Valdez, and Kate Keating. I know that each of you put in so much work behind the scenes that I'll never see, and I'm eternally grateful.

To my usual "thank you" suspects—your love and encouragement meant the world to me during the *Growing Pangs* publishing process. Thank you to members of my family who have rooted for my work and been emotionally supportive over these past few years. Annie and Matt, you are the best siblings a gal could ask for. Shelly, my twin from another life, I'm so grateful for your friendship. Thank you to Destiny, Mai, Nicole, Hilary, Sara, Kayla, Ariana, Laura, Megan, Bob, and Vicki for being plain fantastic during a tough year and its aftermath. You are rock stars, and I feel so lucky to know each one of you.

Alli, you saw me through this entire project, from beginning to end. You were there to comfort me during the tough times, to jump up and down when I got good news, and to cheer me on through every revision and decision. Plus, you are, quite simply, the best. I still can't believe I get to call you my wife.

Writing this story involved many long, intense reflections on my past, and one of the strongest emotions that bubbled up during that process was gratitude for the people whose stories intersected with mine as I was growing up. We might have known each other for only short seasons of my childhood, but you left indelible impressions on me. Thank you for those memories.

Finally, thank *you*, reader, for reading this novel! You are the reason I tell stories, and it's been an honor to share this one with you.

—Kathryn

I would like to offer sincere thanks to Kathryn Ormsbee for sharing this heartfelt story and for allowing me to participate in the telling of it.

Gratitude also to April Ward, Polo Orozco, and Shana Corey for their guidance and expert management on this project. The whole process was a delight, and their notes and edits made the final product stronger.

Huge kudos to colorist Bex Glendining and flatter Elise Schuenke for the care and talent they applied to the project. Their work really brought the line drawings to life, and I'm so grateful for their contribution to this book.

To Sara Crowe for excellent agenting and for checking in when I went quiet.

And to my wife, Amy Luo, for mostly tolerating my inability to accurately judge how many hours a thing will take.

All the best,
Molly

Kathryn Ormsbee

KATHRYN ORMSBEE is the author of many critically acclaimed middle-grade and YA books, including *The House in Poplar Wood* and *Tash Hearts Tolstoy*. *Growing Pangs* is her graphic novel debut and is inspired by her childhood. Kathryn wrote *Growing Pangs* because it's a story she wishes she'd had when she was Katie's age. She grew up in Kentucky and lives in Oregon with her wife and their dog. Visit her online at kathrynormsbee.com and @kathsby.

Molly Brooks

MOLLY BROOKS is the author and illustrator of the acclaimed *Sanity & Tallulah* graphic novel series and many other short comics. Her art has appeared in numerous national magazines and newspapers including the *Boston Globe* and *Time Out New York*, and she is also the illustrator of the graphic novel *Flying Machines: How the Wright Brothers Soared*. Molly grew up in Tennessee and now lives in Brooklyn, New York, with her wife and cats. Like Kathryn, Molly experienced OCD growing up and says, "I am the kid who needed this book, and that has made it a special joy to draw." Visit her online at mollybrooks.com and on Twitter at @mollybrooks.